RUINED KING

NIGHT ELVES TRILOGY - BOOK 2

C.N. CRAWFORD

CHAPTER 1

ALI

This was how I spent my days now: shackled to a mine cart at the end of a narrow tunnel. Life in the crystal mine—just me, my shovel, and my thoughts. I dug into the pile of rock. With a grunt, I dumped the chunks of granite into an old mine cart. Then, I jabbed the shovel into the pile of rock again. I'd been here three weeks and hadn't uncovered a single crystal yet. I wasn't sure they even existed at this point. So, it was just me and the dust and the granite.

My only consolation was that Barthol wasn't here with me—that my brother was free, at least.

Lift, dump, lift, dump, lift, dump ...

Sweat dripped from my brow, and my muscles ached. Ahh, here, I had the pleasure of an oppressively low ceiling, suffocating humidity, and dust coating every inch of my skin.

Lift, dump, lift, dump ...

I tossed two more shovelfuls into the cart.

When things were really grim, I entertained myself with thoughts of slitting Galin's throat. After all, his betrayal was the reason I was here.

I wanted Skalei, my shadow-blade, desperately. I missed

her familiar steel, the razor-sharp edge that could slice an elf's throat to the bone. That could cut through anything, really. If I had Skalei, I'd hack off my shackles and be on my way to the surface in seconds. I'd literally carve a path if I had to. A few dead guards would be a small price to pay for my freedom.

Too bad all I had was a rusty iron shovel. I doubted it could even bash an elf's head in.

Lift, dump, lift, dump …

Rage gathered within me at the thought of Galin. I'd kill him someday. *That* thought perked me up.

I hummed as I worked. Not entirely in tune, but still recognizable: "Single Ladies." The music of the Great Queen Beyoncé, who'd once ruled before Ragnarok.

Sweat mixed with the dust on my body, and I jabbed at the rock pile like my shovel was Skalei delivering the *coup de grace*. Beyoncé represented strength, honor. The very qualities I needed to possess if I were to achieve my destiny. I'd make up for allowing Galin to trick me into helping him— him, of all people. The vilest enemy of the Night Elves.

I continued to jab the shovel at the pile of stones. I was the North Star. The one destined to free my people. I would escape, retrieve Skalei, and then I would pierce Galin's heart. He was mortal now. I could hurt him. A single stab to the aorta and his blood would pool at my feet. Game over.

Lift, dump, lift, dump …

Dust rose from the rocks, nearly as thick and dark as the anger that clouded my mind. I hummed "Single Ladies" as loud as I dared.

When I saw him again, I wouldn't let his infuriating beauty blind me to what he really was. And when he was dead, I'd feel the sun shining on me again. Because I knew that when his soul was in Hel, I'd finally be free of him, redeemed in the eyes of my people.

"Ali?" a voice cut in, wrenching me from my daydream.

Even without looking over my shoulder, I recognized the voice. Her name was Hulda. Technically, she was another Night Elf prisoner like myself, but while I was becoming thin and wiry from shoveling rocks, Hulda was healthy and beautiful from all the time she spent eating raspberries and cream and pies. While most of us starved, the guards gave her extra food and easy work. In exchange, she fed them information. She spied on us.

Unencumbered by leg shackles, she sauntered up to me. She leaned over my shoulder, crowding my physical space, and looked at my rock pile through tired eyes. "Whatcha doing?" she asked, as if shoveling rocks was some sort of novel task she'd never heard of before.

"It's this amazing new hobby I have called *shoveling rocks*. Really tones up the arms and the abs. Want to try?" I slung another shovel-full of granite into the mine cart.

"Why were you making that horrible noise?"

"What are you talking about?" If there was one thing I'd learned since they sent me down here, it was to never admit guilt. It actually made the punishment worse.

"You were moaning. It sounded like words, but I couldn't understand them." Hulda's eyes narrowed. "Was that horrific noise supposed to be singing?"

Not sure I liked her tone. "Hulda, I'm sure you have more important things to do than review my musical talent."

I didn't bother to ask why she was here. I knew the guards had sent her. They kept close tabs on me. Made perfect sense. It wasn't every day a Night Elf committed high treason.

My entire life, I'd been raised to believe it was my role to kill Galin, Prince of the High Elves. I was the North Star—destined to lead my people to freedom. And with every breath I'd taken, I believed our emancipation began with that bastard's death. It was my job to make it happen.

But somehow, after a long-ass journey together, Galin had managed to convince me otherwise. According to his pretty stories, I had it all wrong; his death wouldn't free my people. And the magical wall that had trapped us underground wasn't the wall of a prison—oh *no.* It was there to keep us safe.

Or so he said.

When I'd left him, he'd promised to help me, that he was going to be our savior now. We'd had a deal, I thought. I'd helped him and he'd help me. He'd make it all right.

Except that was a giant crock of shit, because of course it was.

Never trust a High Elf. They feast on deceit, bathe in lies, and sleep on a bed of mendacity.

I gritted my teeth, shoveling the granite with an aggressive ferocity usually reserved for the insane.

Instead of coming to help me, as promised, Galin had personally seen to it that I was locked up, under the ground. Three weeks ago, he'd sent a letter to the Shadow Lords. He explained that I had lied to them. He said I was a traitor, and that we'd traveled together. He told them I had helped him escape the Citadel. It was information only Galin could know.

He expected me to die here, because that's what people did in the mines. He'd ratted on me, knowing what the consequences would be. Because, apparently, I was an inconvenience. He had no intention of helping the Night Elves. He never had.

And as I sweated down here in the dark, shoveling granite, I started to realize he'd probably lied about everything. That story about how I didn't need to kill him to free my people? Another crock of shit. Pretty lies, as pretty as his face.

And perhaps—just as I'd been taught my entire life—our freedom began with his death.

He thought I'd die down here, but I wouldn't give him that satisfaction. No, the Night Elves would fertilize our new lands with his blood.

After Galin's treacherous letter, my punishment had been swift and brutal. No trial. No chance to defend myself. The Shadow Lords simply sent a contingent of guards to my house and seized all my belongings. They took everything: my iPod, my vergr crystal, even Skalei.

The guards dragged me into Sindri. I fought them, but there were too many. They pinned me down, and then the Lords used a magical spell to pull the runes from my forearms. I could shout for Skalei as much as I liked, but she wouldn't come for me anymore. Trust me—I tried.

And finally, they banished me to the Audr Prison Mine.

No one had spelled it out yet, but once they'd used up my strength in the mines, once I'd been driven mad by the confinement, I imagined they planned to execute me. People tended to lose their minds down here.

Except I wasn't growing weaker. Despite losing weight, I was getting strong with all this shoveling. And I knew I wouldn't be down here forever.

"Ali, you're slowing down." crooned Hulda. "The guards will come if you don't shovel fast enough. They're still annoyed about what you did yesterday."

Yesterday, a guard had smacked my ass. So I did what any assassin would do: I broke his wrist and his nose before they pulled me off him.

"Oh, that? It was an accident," I lied. "I just fell into him."

"Sure."

Hulda skulked away, down the tunnel that led to the prisoners' quarters. When I finished shoveling my pile of rocks, I could join her. Drink a little water, slurp down some gruel, then sleep. I'd let my body rest until tomorrow, when there'd be a fresh pile of rock to move. But this time wasn't wasted. Every time I lifted that shovel, I was only growing stronger.

I hefted the shovel and bore down. Dust filled the air as I hurled chunks of granite into the mine cart. I was certain of only two things: I was going to escape, and I was going to kill Galin. Because not only had he betrayed me, but he was now powerful as Hel—and I was sure he was conspiring to keep the Night Elves trapped forever, where he'd put us in the first place.

Killing him would be the first step to gaining our freedom once and for all. Then Gorm, then the rest. I'd pick them off, one by one.

CHAPTER 2

GALIN

*E*arlier in the night, a storm had rolled in. Now, a cold wind rattled the windowpanes. I cracked my knuckles, then loosened my shoulders. Everything was ready. For nearly three weeks, I'd worked in secret to prepare this spell, and I had one chance to get it right. When I glanced in the mirror, I made sure the runes were painted exactly as they should be on my bare chest, the runes glowing in the dim light.

The embers in the hearth were the only thing lighting my room, allowing dark shadows to collect in the corners. My furnishings were sparse—a bed, a sofa, and an old mirror hanging on the wall. I caught a glimpse of my reflection and found myself still startled at my appearance, after a thousand years of looking like someone else. I was alive, a High Elf now. My hair and eyes were gold, my skin tan.

I got up and checked my door. It was locked, just as it had been five minutes earlier. Convinced I wouldn't be disturbed, I returned to my desk and whispered, *"Finnask."* The tabletop shimmered, then transformed from a pile of books and papers into a meticulously organized workbench.

Honestly, there wasn't much: a few jars of herbs, some scavenged bowls and cups, a cluster of tallow candles. Not my usual setup, but my glass alembics and cucurbits had all been destroyed when the High Elves raided my home in Cambridge. The only things I'd managed to save were my grimoires, which I'd magically hidden. Still, I had what I needed to remove the Helm of Awe. Perhaps it stopped me from trying to hurt my family, but nothing stopped me from trying to take it off.

Still, the blasted circlet remained affixed to my head. If I so much as touched a finger to it, it zapped my brain. It wasn't just that I couldn't hurt King Gorm, it was preventing me from rejoining Ali. I could open a portal into the Shadow Caverns, but as soon as I tried to cross into it, bolts of white hot magic sizzled into my skull. Try as I might, the helm had kept me in the Citadel.

In the last three weeks, one thing had become clear: I'd exchanged one prison for another. I might have a soul again, but my body was not my own. I had no free will.

But after tonight, things would be different.

I'd collected all the tools and ingredients for a salve of unbinding. I had horse hair from the stables, mugwort and nettle from the Citadel's kitchens—I'd even pinched a small piece of ambergris from the vanity in Revna's room—something she used to soften her skin, I think.

I arranged the ingredients before me, going over the protocol a final time.

IN AN EARTHEN POT, melt sea-incense, powders of snakes-bane, the oldest herb, and Sleipnir's hairs. Apply the salve with Odin's plume. When all is prepared, sing the song that frees.

. . .

ALREADY, the runes on my chest glowed brighter. Scribing *kaun*, the rune for fire, I lit the candles. As they guttered in my drafty room, I warmed an old, broken teacup in their flames. Carefully, I placed the ambergris in the makeshift crucible. It melted slowly, emitting a musky aroma.

Next, I added the rest of the salve's ingredients: snakesbane, the oldest herb, and Sleipnir's hairs—or, more simply, nettles, mugwort, and horse hair. Carefully, I swirled them with the end of a raven's feather—Odin's plume—until they formed a greenish liquid. After a minute or so, I sniffed the liquid experimentally. It smelled of pine and earth.

Finally, using a fresh raven feather, I dabbed the salve around the edge of the helm. I held my breath, expecting a magical zap to shatter my consciousness, but none arrived.

The salve applied, I slowly began to incant the words to the unbinding spell. As I chanted, the leftover liquid in the crucible began to glow with a green light. When I spoke the last word of the spell, it flashed, nearly blinding me.

Quickly, I crossed to my mirror. Just as I had hoped, the salve glowed brightly along the edge of the helm, too, and the runes on my chest lit up like stars.

"This better work," I murmured. I reached for the helm, but as my fingers touched the gold, a bolt of searing heat cracked open my mind. I doubled over, gripping the table, and a voice rang in my skull.

"I pledge my life, my ambitions, my desires, and my soul to Gorm, King of the High Elves."

THE WORDS OF MY OATH.

Disappointment tore me apart. The spell had failed. I

remained under my father's thumb, trapped within the walls of the Citadel. And that meant I could not get to Ali. Would she imagine I'd abandoned her?

When the pain subsided, I straightened. There had to be another way.

I was not going to give up. This was only a minor setback. I'd given Ali my word. I'd promised her that I'd come for her, and so I would do whatever it took to get to her.

For a thousand years, as a lich, my past had been erased from my mind. But now that my soul was returned, my memories had come roaring back. And, I now remembered what I'd once been: the most terrifying warrior of the High Elves. With magic and my sword, I'd served the gods by cutting down my enemies one by one, following my fate. In my vision of the future, it looked as if I would become a fearsome warrior once again—a king, even.

I'd seen the vision—the crown on my head, the royal scepter in my hand. I would take the throne of the High Elves, the throne that was rightfully mine. I'd foreseen it.

The only thing that twisted my heart was that Ali hadn't been in the vision.

There must be a way to change my fate, to make it so that she ruled by my side as my queen. A loophole of some sort. Anything to have her with me again.

Whatever it took, I would do it.

* * *

SIX HOURS LATER, I peered blearily at a manuscript. My head still throbbed from the Helm of Awe's magical attack. More than anything, I wanted to sleep, but I had to keep working. I had to convince Gorm that nothing was amiss, that I was willingly doing his bidding. That I had no plans to end his long life.

The morning sun was rising, staining the sapphire sky with rosy gold. I looked up from my writing desk. Spread out below me were the ruins of Boston, entombed in a thousand years of ice and snow. The sight pierced my heart; the icy light was enough to remind me that the ravages of Ragnarok endured. I'd been dead and imprisoned for a thousand years, which meant it felt like only yesterday that the world had been alive and the gods had still ruled.

Only yesterday the world had had meaning. Now, we had to make our own.

I refocused on the page, staring at the beige vellum as I carefully inscribed a rune on the paper. It was a tricky fortification spell. A thousand interlocking symbols that together created a powerful barrier.

After I finished inking the rune, I put down my quill and rubbed my eyes. It took all my mental capacity to see how the runes connected, building and supporting one another like the stones of a castle wall. Each had to be carefully placed, taking into account their strengths and weaknesses. Together, they became unbreakable.

As I lifted my quill to begin the next rune, a loud knock on my door interrupted me.

"Odin's arse," I cursed under my breath as I crossed to the door. Opening it revealed the smirking face of my sister, Revna. Her shimmering platinum hair cascaded over a green gown that probably cost more than the entire Night Elf economy.

"Galin, are you almost finished with the spell father ordered?" she asked as she slipped past me, into my room.

"How lovely to see you, dear sister. Always a pleasure." My voice dripped with sarcasm.

She ignored me, plopping herself onto my sofa. She had brought an orange with her and began to peel it. "This sofa is comfy. Where did you get it?"

"As much as I always enjoy our chit-chats, I'm afraid I have work to do."

"I'll be quiet as a mouse," Revna flicked a piece of peel onto my floor. "I like watching you work." She cocked her head. "Particularly without your shirt on, with the candlelight sculpting those fine muscles.

I said nothing.

"We're only half-siblings," she ventured after a moment. "It's been a thousand years, so we hardly feel like brother and sister anymore."

I clenched my jaw, disturbed by where she might be going with this.

"In the old days, the monarchs always married their relatives to keep the bloodlines pure."

Another involuntary shudder. "Is this a personal challenge to see if you can make me vomit in record time? Perhaps you can try your charms on our lovely brother Sune."

"You haven't seen a woman in nearly a thousand years while you were in prison. Oh, except that little tunnel runt." She gave a dramatic shiver. "Anyway, Sune is not as fun as you."

"Fun? I'm a lethal warrior who spent the past thousand years as an imprisoned lich. *Fun* is not one of my strengths."

Revna rolled her eyes. "Fine. Sexy. Don't you remember all the women who would try to sleep with you back before Ragnarok? You never really liked any of them, but they followed you like lovesick puppies. I'm sure you bedded plenty of them. But none of them were your equal, like I am. Don't you remember—you were known as the Sword of the Gods, fearsome and beautiful. I never got a nickname like that, which seems a major oversight. You and I are equally paired, and now that your soul is returned, I find you appealing."

"Well, this has been a disturbing few minutes, but I must get back to my work. Would you like to go out through the door or the window?"

"Oh, my lovely brother. That *manacle on your mind*"—she made air quotes—"will stop you from defenestrating me any time soon."

"Pity."

Revna's eyes narrowed slightly, her calculating side revealing itself at last. "So, how much of your past do you remember?"

Why was she asking that? "What do you mean?"

"Do you remember me?"

"Unfortunately, yes." *Horrible then, horrible now.*

Still, I studied her. She did look almost the same as before. It was hard to believe she was over a thousand years old, but once elves reach maturity, they age very slowly. King Gorm was nearly nine thousand years old, and he looked barely older than a fifty-year-old human.

Revna's fingers dug into the orange, and juice dripped onto my sofa. "Do you remember how you became cursed?"

Most of my past life was clear as day—the battles, the blood, the glory. The spells I'd conducted in the mountains. It was only the last few years before I'd died that were hazy. I knew that I'd built a magic wall to protect the Night Elves, but in the centuries that had passed, the details had faded away. "I think the curse burned away some of my memories," I finally answered.

Revna's eyebrows flicked upwards. "Well, that explains quite a bit."

"What are you talking about?"

Instead of answering, she walked across the room to stand next to me. The way her eyes lingered on my body had me reaching for a shirt.

"So, what does this fortification spell do?" she asked. "The one father is so keen on."

"I'm sure you know. It will stop the Night Elves from trying to break free, by strengthening the wall. It will stop them from raiding Midgard." In this, at least, my father and I had a common goal. If a battle erupted between the Night Elves and the High Elves, it wasn't our side that would lose.

Revna's tone sharpened. "Why don't you compose a slaughtering hex—something to do away with them for good?"

How about I lock you in a dark prison forever once I become king?

King Gorm and I had just fought bitterly over this very question. Just a few weeks ago, he had asked me to destroy the Night Elves once and for all. With the military campaign against the Night Elves stagnating, he desperately wanted me to design an apocalyptic magical weapon for that purpose.

While I still had this thing on my head, I had to keep him reasonably satisfied, but I couldn't help the High Elves overrun the Shadow Caverns. Fortunately, while the crown kept him protected from my wrath, it didn't allow him to physically control me. So, the wall would remain. I was happy to keep the High Elves from advancing on the Night Elves.

That was my one goal, now. A successful attack on the Night Elf realm could mean Ali's death.

I tried not to think of her too often; she disrupted my focus, and that would only delay my return to her. But the very effort of banishing her from my consciousness brought her beautiful face into my mind. Hair the color of snow; eyes that shone like moonlight on water; skin that had never seen the sun, smooth and unlined. … My heart ached to see her again.

"Well?" Revna snapped, bringing me back to the present.

"Wouldn't it be better to just slaughter them, rather than expend all this energy trying to keep them contained?"

"Revna," I replied coldly. "You do remember, long ago, how easy it was for me to kill those around me? As you have pointed out, I can no longer do that. But are you so sure that will always be the case?"

She paled. "Fine. I'll leave." She walked to my door, back stiff. I was just turning back to my work when she spoke again in a fluting voice. "I almost forgot. Father told me to tell you that we're having a meeting after dinner. He said not to be late. But I should warn you. He has news that will make you want to murder him." She cocked her head. "Too bad you can't."

CHAPTER 3

GALIN

The pair of guards were dressed in light armor, and they each gripped a wand buzzing with a killing hex. Together they flanked a set of gilded doors. Even though I was next in line to the throne, they glared at me. Probably because I'd eaten some of their friends while in prison. Not that I particularly cared.

"I have a meeting with the king," I announced as I approached.

Without speaking, the guards pushed open the golden doors.

The resplendent doors were only a prelude to the inside of King Gorm's apartment. My father's approach to interior design could be summed up in one word: *gold*. If it could be gilded, it was: the chair legs, the drapes, the velvet of the sofa. Even the toilet seats in the bathrooms were gold plated.

Only the ceiling had been spared, and that wasn't saying much. It was lavishly painted with frescoes of Elfheim: snow-capped mountains, primeval forests, and golden-haired elves in varying degrees of undress. Perhaps *three* words were needed to describe my father's approach to interior design: *gold and nudity*.

Instead of ruling to protect the best interests of his people, Gorm served only to enrich himself. In the ancient days, traitorous kings had been killed by being thrown from a tower. I thought that would be a fitting end for him.

"You're late." My father's voice tolled like a church bell as I stepped inside.

He wore his usual shining robes and crown. At his hip hung the only non-gold metallic object in the room. Levateinn, a shimmering silver wand that had once belonged to the god Loki. That wand had saved me, but it had also forced me into my current situation.

Flanked by Revna and Sune, the king stood with his back to a row of massive windows. The remains of Boston's frozen skyline spread out behind them, a constant reminder of what had been lost.

I remembered how Boston had looked before Ragnarok. Sunlight had sparked off the water of the Charles River, Newbury Street had bustled with shoppers, and crowds of Red Sox fans had swarmed Fenway Park most every weekend. Granted, the Red Sox fans had been irritating, but I'd have been willing to tolerate them again if it meant smelling fresh grass and hearing birds sing again.

Now, the river had long since frozen solid, and the only balls thrown in Fenway were made of snow. Even Boston's iconic skyscrapers had crumbled under the weight of Ragnarok's frosty embrace. Only the Prudential Center remained standing, an ice-encrusted reminder of a warmer time.

"The spell?" the king prompted.

"I have it. It will keep the Night Elves from breaking free of their dark caverns." I strode towards my father, ready to press the parchment into his hands, but he stepped back.

Even with the helm on, I scared him.

It was instinct, and he was right to fear me. I was, after all, the most powerful sorcerer alive, and he had tried to kill me, then thrown me in a prison for a thousand years without a soul.

"Sune will take that," he said curtly. "I've been thinking we need a new approach to the problem of the Night Elves."

Revna's eyes flashed with excitement, and Sune grinned. Icy fear began to crawl up my spine. That was a strange sensation; one I'd never felt until I'd met Ali. I'd never worried about my own life, but I feared for hers.

"What new approach?" I snarled.

Revna cut in, positively bursting with glee. "We're going to call for a Winnowing!"

Fear now stiffened my back. A Winnowing was a form of combat that would take thousands of lives—Night Elf and High Elf alike. What if Ali were chosen to fight? "Have you lost your minds? We can't have a Winnowing now. Think of how many people would die."

"Why would you be afraid?" asked Revna. "We've all seen you in battle. The Sword of the Gods could kill all the Night Elves in just a few minutes." Then, she added, "That is, if he *wanted* to."

"That's right," Gorm said, not noticing or not caring about Revna's tone. "This is strictly an opportunity to destroy the Night Elves once and for all."

Never had I regretted anything more than I regretted wearing the helm at that moment. If I could get it off, all three of them would be dead within moments.

As if sensing my anger, the king moved even farther away from me.

"You can't just call for a *Winnowing*."

Gorm's pale eyebrows crept up his forehead. "I thought you'd be excited. A Winnowing is a chance to prove your worth. And you did always love killing, if I remember correctly."

"Only to serve the gods. To serve a greater purpose, and because Wyrd demanded it."

Another step back. Did he realize he was doing it? "This is a greater purpose. To show the world our power. Besides, you said this fortification spell will keep the Night Elves at bay. We should have plenty of time to hold a Winnowing without any of them escaping."

"The Night Elves will never agree to it." Gods, I could only hope so.

"Oh, but they have," my father said, smiling smugly. "It's already decided. I have sent word to the Lords of the Shadow Caverns. They have accepted my offer. The slaughter will begin in three days."

My jaw tightened. "Why would they agree to this? It will be a massacre."

Gorm shrugged. "They have no other choice. They rely entirely on one form of food—their mushrooms. But the mushrooms are blighted, you see. They are starving. Hundreds of children have already died, and they seem rather sentimental about that."

I wanted to strangle him. Darkness clouded my mind, and ice-cold rage. I needed to get to Ali.

I turned away from him, stalking out of the room without waiting for a dismissal. Ali was in danger. I had to warn her.

CHAPTER 4

ALI

Despite the grueling work and terrible food, it was sleep that I dreaded most. Every night, horror filled my dreams.

The nightmare was the same each night. Galin would come for me in the caves. Golden hair and eyes shining, he'd stand before me, shirtless, with the dim light sculpting his muscled chest. He never spoke—it was worse than that. He simply flashed me a sly, cruel smile. His eyes twinkled with amusement, as if he knew with complete certainty what would come next.

I'd tried everything—fighting, running, even hiding—but I could never escape him. He'd always find me, still flashing that lazy smile. Smelling like wood smoke and sage, he'd murmur words to me in a deep, purring voice, though I was never able to make out what he was saying.

In the nightmare, my skin would heat, and an ache would build within me. And I found myself compelled to move closer to him, to wrap my arms around him, burning with need. He'd lift my skirt, kiss me hard, and take me against a stone wall, and I'd know that I'd failed. Again. That I'd given in to the cruel beauty of my worst enemy.

I'd wake with a racing heart, horrified at myself but relieved to be alone.

Here in the mines, I'd learned even more about what a monster he was, listening to the stories from the days before Ragnarok. In battle, he was known to leave entire legions dead, their blood staining the snow, carnage around him.

He'd moved with a divine rage, the tales said, imbued with the spirit of Thor. Maybe his power drew me to him. The stories often told of the lovers who'd follow him around, hoping for his attention. Maybe he imagined I'd be the same. When I saw him again, I'd make sure he understood I wasn't.

When I woke, I lay on the cold stone of my prison cell, wondering what in Hel was wrong with me.

I pushed away that terrible thought and stood gingerly, careful not to trip on the shackles that bound my ankles. Around me, I could hear the other prisoners sleeping, smell the stale air of the mine mixed with the stench of dirty bodies.

Quickly, my Night Elf eyes adjusted to the darkness, and after a few seconds, I could see. Not that there was much to look at. The mine tunnel was as dusty and dark as it had been before I'd fallen asleep.

To my right, it curved downward, towards the twisting warren of secondary tunnels where I spent my days. To my left, it rose upwards in the direction of the guard house and the Shadow Caverns. In the center of the tunnel ran a narrow track, the rails the mine carts rode along. Shackled to them, in either direction, were at least a hundred sleeping prisoners.

I stretched my arms over my head as I tried to rid my mind of Galin's sly smile.

A few minutes later, a light flickered, and a guard's voice cut through the darkness. "Wake up!"

Around me, dark forms stirred, coughing and groaning. As the prisoners awoke, a pair of guards began to walk between the cart tracks. One guard pulled an empty cart behind him, while the other carried a long iron rod, which he used to prod a sleeping prisoner. "On your feet!"

When the prisoner didn't move fast enough, he brought the rod down on the prone form. There was a yelp of pain.

"Time to get moving, mine-rats!" That was what they called us. Mine-rats, rock-slugs, ore-vermin. The condemned scum of Night Elf society.

The guards continued along the mine track. One of the prisoners didn't move even after they'd been hit with the rod a few times, and the guard in charge of whacking shouted, "We got a dead one."

My stomach clenched. With a practiced move, the pair of guards tossed the prisoner's body into the formerly empty cart. By the time they'd reached me, they'd hoisted up four more bodies.

Every morning was a reminder that we were expendable, to be used until we died or went mad. No elf lasted more than a year or two in the Audr mines. Death in darkness was the fate Galin had consigned me to—or so he thought.

"Good morning, traitorous whore," said one of the guards as they reached me. I recognized him and the bandage on his nose immediately. This was the elf who'd made the mistake of smacking my ass.

I smiled charmingly. "Morning. Oh, dear. Did you cut yourself shaving?" I asked.

"Bitch—" The guard started to lunge for me, but his companion held him back.

"Not now!"

The guard with the injured nose growled something at

me under his breath, but he followed his partner down the line of prisoners.

When they reached the end, they turned around and began dragging the mine cart full of bodies back towards the guard house. This was unusual. Typically, when the guards reached the last prisoner, they would unlock our shackles so we could work.

"What's going on?" called out a prisoner.

"Warden wants to see you vermin in the prison yard."

Around me, whispers rose, echoing off the stone walls. Something was up.

The yard was the remains of an old vergr crystal deposit that had been emptied years ago, leaving a cavernous room that could easily fit a few thousand elves. We were supposed to visit the yard once every week for exercise like they do in most prisons, but they never took us. In fact, the only time I'd been to the yard was when I'd passed through on my first day in the mine.

When the guards reached the top of the tunnel, they finally released the magical bindings on our shackles. As I began to trudge up after them, Hulda appeared at my side.

"What's going on?" she whispered. Apparently, whatever was happening was beyond her pay grade.

"I don't know."

"Do you think they're planning on punishing someone?" Hulda's eyes gleamed with excitement.

"Maybe."

Whatever they had planned, I was already envisioning how I might escape during it.

CHAPTER 5

ALI

The guards led us into the yard and lined us up in front of an old gallows. It was a massive wooden scaffold with enough room for five nooses. I shivered at the sight of it.

"Maybe they're going to hang someone," whispered Hulda excitedly.

"You are far too enthusiastic about that prospect." I was trying to ignore her, but my stomach clenched anyway. I'd assaulted a guard. If anyone was going to be executed, it would likely be me.

The gallows were ancient. With no access to the sun, trees couldn't grow in the Shadow Caverns. This meant that anything made of wood had to have been built before Ragnarok—a thousand years ago, when my people had lived free under the sun and the stars.

Around us, prisoners whispered, and eventually, a guard yelled, "Quiet!"

Silence descended as the warden ascended the steps of the scaffold, flanked by a pair of guards holding iron batons.

The warden was a thin elf with close-cropped silver hair and a narrow nose.

He stepped to the edge of the scaffold and held out his hands. "Prisoners, you have been brought here for an important announcement."

Then, he stepped back and crossed his arms across his chest. Ten seconds, thirty, a minute passed. He didn't speak again.

"What's going on?" whispered Hulda.

I shook my head. "No idea."

The warden leaned over and spoke quietly in one of the guards' ears. The man shrugged. I was starting to get the impression that *no one* knew what was happening.

"Tell us where you got that ugly face!" shouted a prisoner near the end of the line.

The pair of guards spun in the direction of the voice.

"Who said that?" demanded the warden.

There was no response. We prisoners might be bold, but we weren't stupid.

The warden and his guards stood there for another minute, and I stared at the gallows, trying not to imagine what it would feel like to die there.

Another shout rang in the darkness: "Cat got your tongue, warden?"

Before the warden could answer, the air behind him began to shimmer with dark magic that had an oily sheen, and my breath caught at the sight. With an electric crackle, the magic rapidly expanded. For a long moment, it hung there like a tiny black hole until a robed figure stepped through.

Instinctively, I whispered, *"Skalei,"* under my breath, but of course, my blade didn't appear.

Around me, prisoners gasped. Hulda's mouth fell open. Even the warden, who must have known this was going to happen, looked surprised. This type of powerful magic was reserved for the upper echelons of Night Elf society. Most Night Elves had never even seen a spell performed.

The robed figure stepped to the edge of the scaffold, pulling back their cowl of thick, gray fabric. I recognized Thyra, one of the three Shadow Lords. Slung over her shoulder was a matching gray satchel. She looked even more stooped and aged than she had a few weeks ago.

"Prisoners of the Audr Mines," said Thyra in a surprisingly clear voice. "I have an important announcement that affects us all, from the Shadow Caverns all the way down to the prisoners in the blackest tunnels. We have negotiated an armistice with the High Elves. For the next month, there will be no hostilities."

My heart leapt as a low cheer erupted from the line of prisoners. This was exceptional news, even if it didn't do much to help us personally. Our families would be safe. In the thousand years of our confinement under the earth, the High Elves had never stopped trying to ruin us. If they'd agreed to a truce, it was a potentially giant breakthrough.

Or, as I quickly started to suspect, a trick.

A suspicion that Thyra immediately confirmed. "However, the High Elves have called for a Winnowing."

At these words, gasps arose. It had been a thousand years since the last Winnowing.

"And you agreed to this?" the warden blurted out, his nostrils flaring with fear.

Thyra's tone was grave. "Something drastic must be done to change our circumstances. This year, our mushrooms are blighted. It's not only prisoners who are starving. We are all starving. Your families have no food. The great High Elf sorcerer Galin has returned. His magic is already strengthening the wall. This is our only chance to free ourselves. This is our only chance, and I mean our only chance, to survive."

"What has this to do with *us*? The prisoners are weak. If there is to be a Winnowing, you must send our best fighters. Not these wretches!" The warden was practically yelling at Thyra. If he wasn't careful, it would be his corpse swinging from the beam of oak above his head.

Thyra ignored him. "The terms of the armistice are that *all* elves are to be subject to the Winnowing. Trust me when I tell you I don't want to send convicts and prisoners to the tournament that will define the fate of our people, but that is what we agreed on."

"I don't understand!" the warden nearly shouted. "The purpose of a Winnowing is to kill off the weakest of us. To strengthen our bloodlines. What does it have to do with the war?"

For the first time, Thyra smiled, silver eyes gleaming. "We have agreed on a new set of terms, warden. The tribe with the most remaining elves will rule over the others. If we win, the war is over. The High Elves will become *our* subjects."

A massive cheer rose from the ranks of prisoners, but the warden was having none of it. "Not to put a damper on the fun, but if the High Elves beat us, then we are to be exterminated, I assume?"

Thyra flashed him a sharp look. "Yes, but if we win, we will have dominion over them. We will be able to escape the confines of this prison."

"It must be a trap. King Gorm would never agree to this." I had to give the warden credit; he wasn't stupid.

Thyra glared at him. "What other choice do we have? Our people are starving. They can't eat rocks, and we have nothing else. We will have to win by our wits."

"Sorry, what exactly is a Winnowing?" asked a younger guard.

"Good question." Thyra paused to gather herself. "In the time before Ragnarok, elves held Winnowings to end conflicts between warring factions. Without them, wars could go on for hundreds of years. Back then, we selected the strongest among us. A Winnowing is a grand tournament of death. Three hundred from each tribe fight in a series of contests. Each tribe gets to choose a contest, and the tribe with the most elves alive at the end is the winner. Many die, yes, but not as many as would die from a thousand years of starvation."

My mind whirled. A Winnowing. An opportunity to free the Night Elves from the Shadow Caverns. A chance to kill High Elves, to gain supremacy over them. I was all in. One hundred percent. We'd have to kill Galin first, though, and I knew it would not be easy.

I raised my hand. "I volunteer!"

Thyra held up her hand, shaking her head solemnly. "If we allowed volunteers, we'd be slaughtered. The High Elves have a brutal and well-trained army. Ours is"—she spoke carefully—"less efficient. We negotiated that all fighters would be randomly chosen from all levels of elf society. That's why even convicts will fight in the tournament. This is why I am here."

"And how, exactly, do you intend to choose the contestants?" the warden growled.

"Every able-bodied elf receives a lot. If your lot is marked, you must fight."

"And if we decline?"

"You'll be executed," said Thyra, looking pointedly at the row of nooses.

My hands clenched into fists, my shoulders freezing in a rigid line, it was taking all my will power to stay in line. I *had* to be part of this. It was the perfect chance to redeem myself, to become the North Star that Mom had always thought I'd be.

What if *this* was my destiny?

"I must be part of this!" I shouted.

"Quiet!" shouted the warden. The ends of the guards' iron batons pointed in my direction. "The next inmate who speaks out of turn will get double shifts for a week."

I bit my tongue. Double shifts were a death sentence.

Thyra appeared unfazed by the warden's outburst as she continued, "I have brought lots for everyone in the mines." She pointed to the gray satchel at her feet and spoke to the warden. "Distribute the contents to the inmates, but they are not to open them until I give the word."

The warden bowed deeply as he collected the satchel. Quickly, he passed it to the nearest guard. "You heard the Lord. Distribute these among the inmates. Then take some for yourselves. No one opens their lot until she says so."

The guard leapt from the scaffold, then hurried to the far end of the row of prisoners. Slowly, he walked down the line of inmates. When he reached me, he handed me a small piece of parchment sealed with a blot of black wax.

He moved on to Hulda, then farther along the line of prisoners, as the warden and Thyra watched mutely. When the guard was done, he hurried back to the scaffold.

I stared at the parchment in my hand, which was now the singular focus of my existence. This was my chance at freedom, at redemption. And perhaps revenge for Galin's betrayal. This was my destiny. It took every fiber of my being not to rip it open then and there.

Finally, Thyra spoke. "You may open your lots."

I tore open my paper. I forgot to breathe. My stomach became a bottomless void.

But the page before me was a faded beige, entirely devoid of markings. I had not been chosen. Fate had not worked in my favor.

And you know what? Fuck fate.

Anger rose in my chest. My hand shook. Fate or not, I had to be at the Winnowing.

Next to me, Hulda whispered, her voice trembling with fear, "What color is yours?"

I stared at my paper, disappointment searing me. "White."

Slowly, Hulda turned her parchment toward me. Inside was a smear of clotted blood. Fate had chosen this idiot.

Fate was obviously wrong—because someone like Hulda would not save us.

What happened next wasn't so much a plan as a primal instinct; a series of steps that would get me what I wanted. What I needed. A chance to redeem myself, and to save my people. A chance to keep Barthol safe, and every other Night Elf. This Winnowing needed real warriors, and I was as good as it got down here.

Quickly, I stole a glance at the scaffold. The warden was speaking to Thyra. The guards were inspecting their papers. No one was looking in my direction. Time to put my assassin skills to use.

I spun, lashing my arm like a bullwhip. My fist hit Hulda in the throat.

"Mmgghhh—" She fell, clutching her neck. Her lot fluttered above her like a vermilion butterfly.

I snatched it, crushing it in my fist.

And that is how I deal with fate.

Then, I dropped my unmarked lot onto her quivering form.

My heart rejoiced. I knew then that I would have my revenge. I was one step closer to killing Galin, to becoming the North Star. Even if fate wasn't on my side, I would write my own.

CHAPTER 6

GALIN

I sat at my desk with a fresh piece of parchment spread out before me. As I raised my hand to write, I felt my fingers cramping. My mind was a knot of twisting emotions. Rage, regret—and, worst of all, a sense that I was losing control. That maybe my vision of becoming king would never come to pass, or worse—that I wouldn't have Ali by my side.

I looked up from the paper. In the darkness of night, Boston's buildings spread out before me like the stones of a distant cemetery. Crumbling and broken, they were an ever-present reminder of a better time, a glorious age snuffed out by machinations over which it had had no control. When I had been the Sword of the Gods. Ragnarok had sentenced man and elf alike to an eternally frozen existence, and it still disoriented me.

My fingers tightened on my quill. When I became king of the High Elves, I would find a way to fix this. Turn back the curse, thaw the world. Was this my destiny? Was this my fate?

My spell could wait. Tomorrow, I'd organize the runes

and glyphs, I'd paint them on my chest once more. I'd been up the entirety of the previous night composing the fortification spell. What I needed was sleep.

I pushed my chair back and blew out the candle. I stripped off my shirt, trying not to think of my perverse sister ogling me, then stepped out of my trousers and collapsed onto my bed, one arm thrown over my eyes. Satin and down enveloped me.

I closed my eyes, willing myself to relax. But each one of my muscles was tense, taut. As much as I twisted and turned, I simply couldn't get comfortable. A bed wasn't for me.

I crawled out of bed and onto the floor. Even if the past thousand years seemed like a dream, my body seemed to remember them. After all that time sleeping on stone, my coiled muscles rebelled at the gentle cushion of a mattress. I closed my eyes, then opened them again.

Flames danced along the logs in the hearth, crackling as they burned, but I needed total darkness to sleep. I traced a sharply angled C in the air, muttering, "*Kaun.*" Magic flickered over my bare skin, and the fire went dead.

I closed my eyes again. Finally, darkness, where I now felt most at home, welcomed me. I breathed slowly, allowing my muscles to relax. My aching body yearned for sleep, but I stirred again. I still had another task to complete.

The Helm of Awe clinked on the stones as I shifted position. Revna was right—it was a manacle on my mind. A golden cuff that stopped me from killing the king and all his guards. A chain that kept me from leaving the Citadel.

Almost.

There was one place the crown couldn't follow me. I exhaled deeply, and magic crackled over my skin. Then, I allowed my soul to break free of my body. In an instant, I'd ascended to the astral plane.

I floated in a void. Most would fear this place, since it was so like death. But I'd already been dead. It was blacker than any cavern, inkier than the depths of the sea; I felt smaller than the tiniest of dust motes, a speck in an infinite plane. And yet, it wasn't completely *dark*. All around me, tiny lights flickered like distant stars. The souls of elves.

"Ali," I whispered under my breath.

Like a plummeting meteor, my soul blazed across the astral plane. A light gleamed in the distance, growing brighter and brighter. Even though I'd seen it a hundred times now, the awesome beauty of Ali's soul still astonished me. The perfect complement to my own. The gods were dead, but this was the closest I'd come to divinity.

As our souls neared one another, our connection glowed, the astral manifestation of fate—Wyrd—that bound us for eternity. My heart ached. I could see every detail of my mate's soul, but I couldn't touch or communicate with it in any way.

If fate had declared us mates, why had she not been in my vision of the future, where I'd seen myself as king?

I didn't know, but just being close to her soul eased my despair at the frigid wreck the world had become. I hadn't felt this despair for a thousand years as a lich, but now—alive again—it was drowning me.

If I could visit Ali's soul on the astral plane, that meant she was alive. That I'd saved her from certain death at my father's hands. I'd sacrificed my chance to be with her to ensure she was safe and at home with her people.

A sense of peace enveloped me, and only then did I allow my soul to drift back to my body.

* * *

"Prince Galin!"

A gruff voice roused me from sleep. I cracked open my

eyes. A guard stood above me, grimacing.

"What do you want?" I croaked, my neck stiff and cold. I really needed to stop sleeping on the floor, and I should probably stop sleeping naked if guards were going to barge in here.

"The king has requested your presence at breakfast."

I rubbed my eyes. "I just saw him last night."

"He demands to see you now."

I groaned, crawling to my feet. Towering over the guard, I watched him shrink back from me. He was shaking. "Fuck off while I put some clothes on," I grumbled.

Two minutes later, dressed in a clean shirt and pants, I was following the guard up one of the Citadel's many stairways. I actually felt relatively well rested, my limbs imbued with strength. The floor might be hard, but it was familiar.

When we reached the king's chambers, the guard pushed open the gilded doors, and I followed him inside.

"Prince Galin," he said, announcing my arrival.

Buttery light streamed in from the windows. King Gorm, Revna, and Sune sat at a table laden with food. Plates were heaped with croissants, butter rolls, fruit jellies, and scrambled eggs. The king slathered a croissant with orange jam while Revna and Sune sipped from coffee cups.

My stomach rumbled, and it took me a moment to recognize what hunger was. Hunger for real food instead of blood—another thing that kept disorienting me.

Revna looked me over. "Still sleeping on the floor?"

"It suits me."

"It seems very manly," she said.

"Revna!" Sune's lip curled. "Please tell me you're not flirting with him."

At least my brother and I had that disgust in common. Probably the only thing we agreed on.

Her eyes went wide. "Of course not!"

The king waved at an empty chair, his fingers sticky with jam. I could see it still—the fear in his eyes. He tried to mask it, but it was palpable.

"Sit," said the king. "Sit. Stop arguing. You must try these preserves."

I sat, but didn't take any of the food. "Why am I here?"

"Why are you here?" The king laughed like this wasn't the first time he'd ever invited me to breakfast in a thousand years. "Because you're my son, of course. We're having a family breakfast. I wouldn't dream of excluding you."

Just a happy family here. Never mind that he was trying to kill my mate, that he laughed at the thought of her starving to death. Never mind that I fantasized about severing his head from his body.

"I said, why am I here?" I growled.

I watched as the pale hair on his arms rose, and he seemed to shrink away from me. Even before he answered, I winced as the Helm of Awe began to hum. This close to him, the circlet was hypersensitive to anything even vaguely threatening. The anger in my voice alone was enough to activate it.

"I need you to open this." He pushed a small, folded piece of parchment across the table.

"What is it?"

"It's your lot."

I didn't touch the paper. Was this his plan? Unleash Galin, Sword of the Gods on his enemies?

"For the Winnowing," said the king. "All elves have been given lots so we may choose those who will represent us. We've got the Night Elves exactly where we want them. Your sister struck the terms, as she has a talent for negotiation. The winning tribe will lead all the elves. When we triumph, I will become king of all elves, and the Night Elves will be dealt with once and for all."

Dread snaked up my spine as I thought of Ali. "The Night Elves agreed to this plan?" Was that why she wasn't in my vision? Because she would die?

"They are desperate to be free of their caverns. There's not much food down there. It was easy to convince them a Winnowing was in their best interests when they're watching their children die." Gorm laughed. "I think they believe they may actually win. Can you imagine that?"

I looked at the paper on the table, but still, I didn't touch it. "Why lots?"

"It was their idea. The Night Elves were concerned that we'd only send our best men. They demanded the choosing be randomized for all."

Revna grinned. "But what they *don't* know is all High Elves are required to enlist in the military. We are going to absolutely crush them."

I picked up the folded parchment. I knew Gorm had rigged it, that he wanted me there as his secret weapon. But now, I knew I needed to be there. I needed to protect Ali if she was chosen.

Standing, I ripped it open.

No surprises there. I dropped the parchment on Gorm's plate, then turned to leave.

"What did you get?" Revna's voice tinkled.

"I'm sure you already knew," I growled over my shoulder.

She began to laugh. "Galin, brother, of course you're in the fight. Did you actually think you wouldn't be involved? You're the best fighter we have!" As I walked out, Revna called after me, "And won't it be fun to watch your tunnel-runt die?"

She was wrong.

I would personally slaughter every one of the High Elves before I let anyone lay a finger on Ali.

CHAPTER 7

ALI

When the lots were counted, only five of us had the mark. The warden sent the rest of the prisoners back into the mine, and a pair of guards lugged Hulga off to the infirmary.

Then, they took off our shackles for good.

With the warden and two guards in the lead, we were marched up the long, winding tunnel. No one spoke; I heard only the shuffling of our feet over the rough stone.

We stopped when we reached an opening in the mine. A bit of brighter light glowed on the other side. Freedom.

As I crossed through the opening, my breath caught at the view. We were on an upper slope of rubble surrounding the main cavern. Granite spread out beneath us. In the distance, buildings rose from the stone.

After living in tunnels no wider than my wingspan, the enormity of the main cavern was overwhelming, with stalactites and stalagmites so large they would dwarf Boston's skyscrapers and a ceiling so high it disappeared into a murky gloom. The faraway city lights glittered like thousands of stars.

I'd made it. I was free.

Even hungry as I was, euphoria roared in my chest, and I shouted, "Woooooo!"

I listened to my voice echo, and the other marked prisoners joined me.

"Woooooo! Woooooo! Woooooo!" We howled together like a pack of wolves, the excitement of freedom overwhelming any sense of decorum.

"Quiet," growled the warden, but we ignored him, shouting into the darkness, celebrating our escape.

Maybe we were headed to battle, but this was more than we could ever have hoped for. An opportunity to breathe air free of rock dust, the possibility of redemption, the dream of revenge and triumph. The five of us danced and shouted until the warden ordered his guards to beat us if we didn't shut up.

When we were silent, the warden pointed to the distant tower of the Shadow Lords. "We're to go to Sindri," he said as he started down the sloping, dark hill toward the city.

We followed. On the way down the slope, we marched past slag heaps and dilapidated colliery structures. My fellow convicts kept their mouths shut until we crossed onto a narrow road.

A tall elf fell into step beside me. "What were you in for?" he asked quietly.

He probably already knew. "Treason. How about you?"

He winked. "Been here a week but it feels like years. Theft, smuggling, a little bit of this and that—"

"Quiet," said the warden before the elf could continue.

I rolled my eyes. There was no reason for him to threaten us. We were warriors now, not prisoners. "What are you going to do? Kill us?"

The warden fixed me with his gaze. "I will if you run."

I looked at my fellow convicts. They were dirty and thin. "We won't run. Anything is better than the mines."

The warden pursed his lips and stared at us for a long moment, then turned his back and kept walking.

"Is it true you met *him*?" The tall elf asked me, eyes gleaming. It took me a moment to work out who he meant.

"Galin? Yeah. Unfortunately."

Another elf cut in, "So, what are the High Elves like?"

I couldn't say they were beautiful, with golden hair, that they towered over us. Instead, I said, "Uptight. Most of them speak like they've got flutes up their asses."

The elf sucked in a short breath, and his eyebrows shot up. "You're kidding."

"King Gorm demands your fealty," I said in my best High Elf impression.

"Are you serious? That's how they talk?"

"She's right," said the tall elf. "They sound like utter knobs."

I grinned at him then held out my hand. "I'm Ali, by the way."

"Bo," he replied. "So, how'd you end up in the mines?"

With a sigh, I launched into the story of how I'd literally been to Hel and back. After spending my days alone shoveling rock, it felt great to talk. And by the time I'd finished telling them how I'd descended the Well of Wyrd, we'd reached the fluvial plains. Here, we walked past fields of mushrooms: cremini, portobello, matsutake, and black trumpets. But my stomach clenched with horror as I realized something was very wrong with them. They reeked of something foul, and they were growing withered and green. Diseased. No wonder the Shadow Lords had agreed to the Winnowing. The entire city would die if we didn't do something.

Walking through the fields, my mind slid back to happier

times. Normally, every Night Elf worked in the mushroom farms, even if they had other jobs. The fungi were our main source of food, and it was a community effort to care for them. I'd spent my youth in fields just like these. Spreading spores, checking the mycelium mats, and harvesting mushrooms. I remembered when, as children, my brother Barthol and I would find a puffball mushroom and kick it around like a soccer ball until a foreman told us to stop. I wondered how Barthol was doing now. Was he starving, too?

It felt eerie here, desolate. Normally, there were groups of Night Elves tending the mushrooms. Picking off slugs, collecting spores, doing all the things necessary to keep the life-giving fungi healthy. Now, it was completely deserted.

And worse, as we walked on, we passed the old cemetery, the stones jutting from the ground at odd angles. Now, it was full of fresh, new graves. Row upon row of them, many of them small—children's graves.

Tears stung my eyes. This was the result of our imprisonment here, being trapped by the High Elves. By Galin.

After an hour we came to the first town, though it wasn't much, a small collection of stone buildings. As we approached, excitement welled in my chest. This would be the first time I had seen my fellow countrymen in weeks. But as we followed the road into the village, we found it empty. Deserted. There were no elves to greet us.

"Where is everyone?" said Bo.

"I have no idea," I replied, trying to hide the worry in my voice.

* * *

AN HOUR LATER, we reached Myrk, the largest city in the Shadow Caverns. The hunger was cutting through my stomach so sharply now, I felt half insane.

It seemed like a world of death around me. Normally Myrk was a bustling metropolis of bright storefronts and shouting street vendors. There'd be farmers carting mushrooms, weavers carrying bundles of shimmering spider silk, jewelers in little booths selling gemstones.

Instead it was nearly empty, and a putrid stench filled the air. The few elves we saw moved furtively, slipping into the shadows as we approached.

"Warden," I said loudly, "Where is everyone?"

The warden slowed. "I'm not sure."

"Ali?"

I jumped as someone shouted my name. Then, warmth lit me up.

Dressed in his cave bear coat, my brother charged from across the street, grinning like a maniac.

"Barthol!" I cried.

Barthol put his hands on my shoulders, shaking me with excitement. "I can't believe it's you! I've been out of my mind with worry. I was going to try to break you out of the mines."

"That would have been stupid. How did you know I'd be here? What's going on with the city? Where is everyone?" I couldn't quite believe I was seeing my brother, but I was certain I was smiling as broadly as he was.

Barthol looked around a little nervously. "Everyone knows you got a marked lot. They say the 'traitor-assassin' will fight in the Winnowing—" He cleared his throat. "That's what everyone calls you now."

"Oh, I know. But I've stopped caring what they think. Because I plan to kill Galin as soon as I can," I added. "I will be the North Star, just like Mom said."

He grabbed my arm. "You can't kill him, Ali. He's dangerous."

"So am I." I shook my head and, feeling the warden's eyes

on me, quickly changed the subject. "What's going on in the city? Why is no one out and about?"

Barthol's smile faded, his expression becoming solemn. "Mushroom blight, and now a plague. People are dying left and right."

I felt my stomach drop. A plague was what had killed my parents. In the Shadow Caverns plagues were lethal, traveling effortlessly through the dank cave air. And with no food? We had to break free of the caverns at all costs.

I shook my head. "You shouldn't have come to see me."

Barthol's eyes glistened with tears. "Ali, I had to. You're my only family. You're going to fight in a Winnowing, this might be the last time I see you."

I realized I couldn't fault him, as I knew with certainty I would have done the same.

"I'll be fine," I said squeezing one of his massive shoulders. "I've trained for years to fight in this sort of thing—"

"Keep moving!" the warden cut in.

"Ali," Barthol said hurriedly. "The Winnowing—promise me you'll be careful, right? Try to stay out of the fray."

"Of course I will." *Not a chance.* I sensed the warden approaching. "Look, I have to go—"

Barthol had already wrapped me in another hug. I could smell his cave bear coat, but he felt too thin underneath it.

He released me, and the warden grabbed me from behind. "Get in line, now!" His voice was like a gunshot.

Snarling, I moved along to join the other prisoners.

"Ali, wait!" shouted Barthol, running after me. "Take this." He pressed something into my hands. "You'll love it, I promise. I have complete faith in you."

Only after I'd caught up with the prisoners did I dare open my fingers. I grinned as I recognized the plastic and snarl of white wires. I was holding an antique MP3 player just like the one Galin had given me in the realm of the

Vanir. My heart twisted at the memory. It had felt like we were a team, like we were working together. Maybe when he got his soul back, he'd changed.

I slipped the headphones on and pressed play. The most glorious music filled my ears, and a gasp escaped me. The melody was simple but incredibly transfixing, with a childlike purity that just made me want to smile.

Bopping my head, I hummed along to the tune. Whoever had decided to write a song about baby sharks was an absolute genius.

CHAPTER 8

GALIN

For the hundredth time, I paced the length of my room, from the door to the desk and back again. It was late. I should be asleep, but instead I racked my brain, trying to think of a solution. I wanted to leave, to get to Ali. I had to know that she was okay, well fed. The idea of her starving made me feel insane, like I wanted to burn down the entire Citadel. A fiery rage was growing in me.

I needed to hear her voice again.

After that, the way forward was obvious. I would find her and take her on the run. I would steal a moth and fly us to the bottom of the Well of Wyrd. Then, we would make our way to another realm. Someplace they'd never find us.

The only thing holding me back was the helm. It pressed low on my brow, heavy and metallic. Its very presence felt suffocating.

Still, every spell had a counter spell. There had to be a way to remove it.

I went to my desk and flipped through my grimoires. I found hexes that would freeze an elf's blood solid, dozens of spells to ensure good harvests—but apart from the unbinding spell I'd already tried, there was nothing that might plausibly remove the helm from my head.

In frustration, I gave a low growl.

I started to reach for the helm itself. I could power through the pain and tear it off this time, I was sure. But as my hands neared my forehead, the metal began to vibrate. Heat formed behind my eyes. Any closer and I'd be convulsing on the floor.

Still, that gave me an idea.

There was one thing I hadn't tried. With a little finesse, it might work.

I waved at the runes on my doorframe, magically locking it. Then, I pulled off my shirt and traced *kaun*. The rune glowed on my chest, and instantly, flames erupted from the tips of my fingers. I held my hands before me, fire flickering along my palms, around my wrists. The heat warmed my face.

I'd remove the blasted circlet the *hard* way.

I raised my hands towards my head, and the helm began to hum, buzzing with malevolent magic. I gritted my teeth. The pain would be excruciating, but I had to try. Once I melted the metal, its power would fade, and I would be free. Then I could save Ali, become the king I was fated to be.

I moved my blazing fingers closer to the helm.

Without warning, a jolt of magic staggered me, like a giant hand was squeezing my skull. My body vibrated from the pain, muscles tensing all over.

The air smelled of ozone; I tasted gasoline on my tongue. But worst of all was the voice that tolled in my mind— Gorm's voice intoning the words of the oath I'd made to him.

I pledge my life, my ambitions....

OATHS COULD BE MADE, but they could also be broken. This was a crime against the gods, but they were dead now. And Ali's life meant more to me than an oath.

I began chanting *kaun* over and over. Magic poured out of me, and my hands blazed like the sun. The trick was to melt the helm without touching it.

A second blast of magic hit me between the eyes, dead center of my frontal cortex. My room disappeared in a flash of searing agony. Waves of pain contracted my muscles.

Wavering figures stood over me, shimmering like desert mirages. Gorm and Revna. My sister was reaching for me, trying to stroke my chest. *"You are bound to me forever,"* she whispered.

I pressed my hands against the crown.

I will be free.

Pain engulfed me, vibrating down my limbs, contracting each one of my muscles as my body burned. I was sure I was swimming under the surface of the sun. Agony ripped my consciousness apart, until the only clear thought in my mind was Ali.

Then, the pain faded, and I opened my eyes.

I lay on the stone floor of my room. The rune on my chest had turned black, smoking. I drew in several deep, gasping breaths. Slowly, my vision sharpened.

I lifted one of my hands. Smoke rose from my fingertips.

Had it worked? I staggered to my feet and stepped in front of my mirror.

My collarbone was charred, my hair singed, but on my head—shining, metallic, and completely intact—remained the Helm of Awe.

Except … it felt just a little weaker now. I hadn't pulled it off, and it still controlled me. But I was certain I'd damaged its power.

And if there was one thing every sorcerer knew, it was that every spell had a weakness. A fatal flaw.

More than ever, I was certain I would find a way to rid myself of the helm. It was my destiny.

* * *

THUNK. *Thunk. Thunk.*

Someone knocked on my door. At this hour, it had to be a guard with a request from my father. Then, a second thought occurred to me—could the helm have warned him that I'd managed to damage it?

I pulled on a shirt, covering the smoking rune on my chest before going to the door. When I cracked it open, a petite, cloaked figure slipped past me, into my room.

"You can't come in here—" I began. Then the figure turned, and I gasped.

It wasn't possible. And yet it was. That delicate jawline, the soft lips, the silver hair peeking out from under the hood, the bright silver eyes. My heart slammed against my ribs.

Ali had come to me.

"How did you—"

"Shhh," She lifted a finger to her lips. Then, she rushed for me.

I wrapped my arms around her small body, one hand on her lower back, the other pressing her head to my chest. I felt like my heart might explode with relief. She was soft, warm, and smelled of jasmine and dark chocolate. She looked healthy enough, not starving as I'd feared.

I spoke to her in a quiet voice, attempting to rush through an explanation: "I wasn't able to come to you. The helm has kept me from leaving the Citadel. I've been working to remove it, but the magic is stronger than I expected."

Silver eyes gleaming, she touched my cheek. When she pulled open her cloak, I found that she was wearing a sheer silver dress that showed off *every* curve of her body—her delicate waist, perfect breasts. I slid my gaze down her form, my blood roaring in my ears.

Desire ignited. And yet ... somehow, rational thought intruded. "How did you get here? The Citadel is full of guards. It's not safe for you—"

"I'm a trained assassin," she said with a smile.

"That's not enough of an explanation."

"The Lords sent me to you. They know you want to help us." Gently, she pushed away from me, but she still let her cloak fall open, rendering me practically mute. "Tell me what Gorm's weakness is. What can we use against him?"

I had to tear my eyes away from her just so I could concentrate. I looked out the window as I gathered my thoughts. "Have you been chosen for the Winnowing?" I asked, stealing another look at her.

She shrugged, her silver hair falling in her eyes. "Galin, please, I don't have much time."

"But are you getting enough to eat, Ali? I heard about the blight."

"What's his weakness?"

Vaguely, I wondered why she'd come here in that transparent dress if she wanted answers, because it was deeply distracting. All I could think of was lifting it up around her waist and wrapping her legs around me. The effects of the magic zapping my brain seemed to have put me in a haze, but Ali's beauty wasn't making it any easier to think.

With a great deal of effort, I said, "Gorm believes that a king must lead with fear and violence. He will always take the most vicious, most brutal approach to any problem."

"And you can use that against him?"

"Just put him in a situation where his desire for blood is in opposition with his need for restraint. He'll overextend every time."

"Ah," Ali breathed. "And what of your sister, Revna? Doesn't she advise him now?"

"She does, but her desire for blood is even greater than my father's. He's the one with restraint, not her."

"Why does Gorm hate the Night Elves so much?" she pressed.

I frowned as I thought over the thousand-plus years I'd known my father. "He's always spoken of how he hates the Night Elves. Even when I was a boy, before Ragnarok, he talked constantly of killing them. I think he blamed them for any problems in Elfheim. They were always scapegoats."

I turned to look at her again, my pulse racing. I didn't want to talk any longer.

I stalked closer to her. She backed up against the wall, looking up at me, and I pressed my hands to the stone behind her head. As I leaned in, my eyes were on her lips.

She held her hand up, stopping me from kissing her.

I turned my face slightly. "Ali, how did you get here? And tell me if you are part of the Winnowing."

"I am."

A protective fire burned in me. I'd have to kill my own kind to keep her safe. "Ali, most who fight in a Winnowing die. "

"I'll be fine."

"When I see you on the battlefield," I continued feverishly, "we must pretend to fight, or we will be killed by our own people. But I will use the fight as a chance to speak to you, to get up close."

She gave a little shrug. "We might be busy killing others."

I felt a distance between us, and it made my chest ache

with the emptiness of a world without gods. "What happened after I last saw you?"

"After you sent me back to the Shadow Caverns, I went straight to the Shadow Lords. I told them everything that happened. How we travelled into the Well of Wyrd. How you killed the Emperor of the Vanir …"

Confusion stirred in my chest. "How *I* killed him? I helped, but you delivered the final blow."

Ali shoved me with unexpected force, so hard it felt like she could have broken a rib. "What did you say?" Her expression was suddenly furious. "About the emperor?"

"That you stabbed him to death."

"No." Ali stepped back, her face now a mask of horror, "I must have forgotten."

She stood in the center of my room, swaying slightly. I was starting to wonder if she'd lost her mind since I last saw her. My mind churned, thoughts frantic.

"What is going on?" I demanded. "What happened to you?"

She straightened suddenly. "I must go. My people need me."

"How in the gods' names will you get out of here? You need to stay with me, Ali." I moved in front of the door. If the guards caught her, she would die a painful death.

"Get out of my way, Galin." Her eyes blazed with intensity, madness.

"Have you lost your mind?"

Ali spun away from me, fast as the wind, and ran for the window. Flying over my desk, she smashed through the glass and leapt out into the night air, twenty stories above the earth.

I felt as if the world tilted beneath me, panic stealing my thoughts.

"Ali!" I shouted leaping onto the desk, leaning out over

the broken glass. Terror clutched at my heart as I looked down. I expected to see her clinging to the side of the Citadel, or worse, smashed into the snow twenty stories below.

But what I saw felt worse. A few snowflakes glistened, the lights of Boston twinkled, but there was no sign of the Night Elf.

Ali had simply vanished. I wondered if she'd actually been here at all, or if my soul had yearned for her so much I'd simply imagined her.

Perhaps I was losing my mind.

CHAPTER 9

ALI

As I listened to the baby shark song on repeat, the warden led us straight to Sindri, the towering column of stone where the Shadow Lords lived. A guard stood at the entrance—the same one I'd spoken to when I'd last visited.

"Winnowing?" he asked the warden.

The warden glared. "Yes, I bring prisoners from the Audr Mines for the Winnowing. They have each drawn a marked lot."

Instead of motioning us past, the guard dropped his halberd to block the entrance. "Only the marked may enter. You don't have a lot. You stay here."

"These elves are dangerous criminals—"

"Lord's orders. Release them, and I will escort them inside. You may return to the mine."

The warden grumbled under his breath, but stepped away anyway.

The guard motioned us forward. "This way."

Quickly, we followed him up the winding entrance tunnel. When we reached the main hall, Bo and the other prisoners stared around, awestruck. I didn't think any of them had ever been inside the Shadow Lords' hall.

Just as they had the last time I'd visited, the three Lords sat on their stone thrones. Unlike last time, when I'd faced them alone, elves filled the hall. Young, old, male, and female, they milled around, looking mournful, emaciated.

As we moved further into the hall, Thyra raised her hand. "My warriors! The last of the marked have arrived. We are all assembled."

The elves quieted, turning to face the Shadow Lords.

"I will be brief," Thyra continued. "Each and every one of you have received marked lots. Three hundred have been chosen to represent our kind. Together, you represent the last hope of the Dokkalfar. A great plague has overrun our land. Our people are dying. We need to escape the confines of the Shadow Caverns once and for all."

Her eyes gleamed, and a heavy silence fell over the hall.

"Let me tell you, briefly, what will happen next. Tonight, we follow the tunnels that lead to Galin's wall. In the morning, the High Elves will let us pass into Midgard. We will travel to Boston, where we will fight at sundown. The first contest will be a melee. Three hundred of us versus three hundred of them. It is a fraction of our population to stop the starvation, and I believe it is our last hope. During the first trial, the blood will flow until half remain. Then we will rest until the next contest, and on and on until only thirty elves remain. It is a sacrifice, yes, but without it we risk total annihilation. Most of you will not survive the next week. But do not fear for your souls. A death in battle is a glorious way to die. At the moment you draw your last breath, the valkyries will lift you up and you will live in eternal glory in Folkvangr or Valhalla."

A hundred questions raced through my mind, but I couldn't ask them now. My muscles were tense, and fear mingled with anticipation. This was my chance to kill my oldest enemy—and this was our chance to free the Night Elves. But it could end in disaster.

Thyra continued, "We are looking for advisors among you. Anyone who has been into Midgard and may have intelligence about weaponry, tactics. As we travel, I will be collecting any information I can."

Around me, the crowd of elves began to murmur.

Thyra nodded. "We will leave at once. The way to the wall is long and arduous—"

"Wait!" shouted Bo suddenly.

The Shadow Lord glowered. "Who dares to interrupt me?"

"I just thought— Your Lordship." Bo bowed his head slightly. "I think you should speak to Ali. Midgard has changed over the years, and I believe she knows the High Elves better than any of us."

Thyra's lips thinned. "Anyone but the traitor."

"She has visited the Citadel, met King Gorm—she's even traveled to realms beyond our own."

"She committed high treason," the Shadow Lord said coolly. "She fraternized with the enemy. She helped bring Galin back from the dead. She is the reason we are in this predicament."

Bo was right, though. I had the means to help them—I just had to convince them to let me.

I stepped forward. "You never gave me a trial. You haven't heard my story. But if you want someone who understands the High Elves and Midgard, I'm the closest you've got."

Thyra looked to the other Shadow Lords. Almost imperceptibly, Lynheid inclined her head.

With a long-suffering sigh, Thyra turned back to glare at me. "We will speak later."

* * *

We'd walked for hours, now, making our way through the narrow tunnels that led to the surface. We only stopped to make camp when we'd reached the impenetrable magical barrier that was Galin's wall.

I crouched next to Thyra and Ilvis on a ledge just feet from the wall. As it shimmered darkly above us, I warmed my hands beside a small fire of smoldering coal. Soup bubbled in a cast iron pot above it. All around, the chosen were leaning against walls, resting and eating. Light from torches wavered around the tunnel.

"Hungry?" Thyra asked me quietly.

I nodded, and she ladled steaming soup into an earthenware mug, then handed the mug to me without speaking. I inhaled deeply. Bird's nest with chunks of fried bat wing, my favorite. I took a long sip, then leaned against the wall of the cave and allowed the mug to warm my hands.

It was strange being this close to Thyra and Ilvis. Ilvis was silent, with a deeply wrinkled face he kept hidden under the hood of his cloak. Thyra, on the other hand, sat with her hood pulled back as she studied me with piercing gray eyes.

Up on her throne, she'd seemed distant and aloof, but now that I'd spent the day at her side, I'd learned she was more than that. Certainly, she was quiet, but she was also sharp—a fierce intelligence within a wizened frame.

"I didn't know he was Galin," I said. "I only knew he was a lich. You sent me on a mission into Midgard, and I was captured. The lich got me out. He looked nothing like Galin, and I knew he wasn't a High Elf. I traveled with him because I thought we were retrieving the ring you wanted. I swear to you that I had no idea who he was. I always planned to destroy the wall, and I still do. It's been my dream since I was a little girl. And since Galin sent you that letter, getting me thrown in prison—who do you think wants that High Elf fuck dead more than anyone?"

"Mmmm." Thyra considered me. "Perhaps."

"You will see. I will kill him," I promised. "When do we cross into Midgard?"

"We cross the barrier in the morning," she replied. "Galin's wall will be temporarily lifted."

"And then what?"

"The first contest of this Winnowing is to be held in Boston Common, at the corner of Beacon and Charles Street. We fight at dusk."

"Until three hundred elves remain?"

"Yes."

I rubbed a knot in my forehead. "I realize this is our only hope, but this is a bad deal."

Thyra's eyes narrowed. "We have Wyrd on our side."

I groaned inwardly. Wyrd was starting to seem like bullshit to me. "That's what the High Elves think, too, because everyone tells themselves that. It won't be enough, not when their weaponry vastly outshines ours. We will need to be strategic."

"How so?" Thyra leaned forward, studying me intently.

"Our people are armed with rusty swords and broken shields. The High Elves will be in full plate armor and wielding six-foot broadswords. As soon as the Winnowing starts, they'll charge and cut down half of us before we can even touch one of them. We're going to get slaughtered if we don't have a brilliant plan." I sighed, my mind racing as I tried to come up with a solution. "If I were in charge, I'd lay a trap. Having Wyrd on our side doesn't mean we can't also seize the initiative tomorrow."

Thyra exchanged a look with Ilvis. "Can you be more specific?"

"What if we goad Gorm into attacking us? The High Elves

will charge our position and we'll counter-attack. We can use our vergr crystals to flank them."

Thyra shook her head. "We can't use crystals. The Winnowing rules strictly forbid the use of magic. Even scribing a simple rune is grounds for disqualification."

I shrugged. "So a few of us are disqualified. It's a tactical decision."

"The rules state that for every disqualified elf, an additional two elves from their side must also die. I will not sacrifice the lives of our people in that way."

Balls. "Okay. Forget that." I closed my eyes, working through the possibilities. "What if we armed ourselves with spears?"

She frowned at me like I was a total idiot. "We don't have any spears. There are no trees in the Shadow Caverns."

My mind raced. "Are we allowed to use magic to help in our preparations?"

Thyra pulled a bundle of papers from her satchel. She licked the end of her forefinger, then began flipping through them, muttering under her breath.

"What's that?"

"It's the contract I signed with the High Elves. It contains the rules of the Winnowing." She hummed low in her throat as she read it. Then, she looked up at me. "There's nothing that says we can't use magic in our preparations."

"Did you bring any vergr crystals?"

Thyra nodded. "Yes, but we only have five."

"Can I borrow them and four elves?" I pointed to the shimmering black magic that made up Galin's wall. "What if I lead a small team across the barrier tonight? There are plenty of dead trees in the Common we can use to construct spears. We'll hide them in the snow on the battlefield. Then, when the High Elves charge, we snatch them up and the High Elves impale themselves. I know the landscape. I've been there just recently, and no one else has. I can do this faster than anyone."

Thyra's eyes gleamed in the darkness of the cave. "That could work. However, I will instruct everyone around you to slaughter you if you make an attempt to flee or betray us again."

"Wouldn't dream of it."

"And so I'm clear on the plan," said Thyra, "when you're done, you'll return to tell me exactly where the spears are hidden? Or you forfeit your life in an excruciating manner?"

"I will send an elf back to show you where to find the spears."

"You won't come yourself?"

I bit my lip. "Do the rules say anything about when we can arrive at the battlefield?"

"They do not."

"What if I and the other three of my team conceal ourselves in the snow? Once the battle is underway, we could attack from the rear."

"Only four to attack from the rear?"

I leaned forward, speaking in a whisper. "More of an assassination, focused on Galin. He's the biggest threat among them. His father had him locked up for a thousand years, like a weapon he was waiting to use, instead of killing him. He's the Sword of the Gods. The prince is the real threat here. If we sneak up from behind when he's not expecting us, it's our best chance."

Thyra continued to sip her soup as she mulled over my words. At last, she answered, "I will choose your team so that I can be certain they are watching you. They will report any deception back to me."

"Deal."

"And one more thing." Thyra reached into her bag. "I believe this is yours."

As she pulled her hand back out, I gasped, and a smile curled my lips. A blade glistened in her hand. Black as the darkest cavern, sharp enough to slice an elf's throat to the bone.

This was my blade. My dearest friend. Skalei.

Thyra glared at me. "Now, hold out your forearms so that I may carve the binding runes again."

CHAPTER 10

GALIN

I stood on a small knoll overlooking Boston Common, the ancient park in the center of the city. In its earliest incarnation, the Common had been a burial ground for the Wampanoag people. In the Puritan era, it had been a cow pasture and site of the witch-hanging tree. Later, the British had used it as a camp for their soldiers during the American Revolution. It was only in the early years of the 19th century that the city had designated it a park.

Now, for the first time in its long history, it would be a battlefield.

I still wondered if I'd see Ali here, or if my visit from her had been a figment of my imagination.

Next to me, Revna shifted nervously. "Where are they?"

"They'll be here soon." My voice was quiet. I fought the urge to run across the Common, to search for Ali. I had to be patient and trust that she would be fine.

I glanced at the sky, now tinged with the faintest stain of peach. Dusk was almost upon us. If the Night Elves didn't show up before the sun set, they'd forfeit the Winnowing entirely. And if that happened, I was certain Gorm would use it as an excuse to destroy them once and for all.

Behind us, the sun dipped lower, and shadows darkened the alleys between the townhouses along Beacon Street. I rolled my shoulders, trying to relieve the tension in my muscles. If this were a thousand years ago, my body would be electrified with battle fury. I'd already be looking forward to dipping my sword in enemy blood, dedicating each death to Freyr. As a lich, I'd forgotten the gods entirely for a thousand years. And now their loss had come roaring back to me.

But Freyr was dead; none of this meant anything anymore, and my mate was out there, in danger. The thrill of battle was as dead as the gods, and I only wanted Ali in my arms again.

If we won the Winnowing, my father would destroy the Night Elves. But if we lost, I'd be the first one the Night Elves tried to kill when they came into power. They wouldn't succeed, but I'd have to exile myself.

The only question was if Ali would join me.

I clenched my jaw, trying not to think about her. She'd visited me then left, literally throwing herself out my window. Part of me wondered if some strange magic was at work, but she'd seemed as solid as the floor beneath my feet.

"There." Revna pointed into the distance. "Do you see them?"

I squinted, wishing, not for the first time, that I had a bit of Ali's Night Elf eyesight to help see in the dark. At this distance, I could discern only shadows—but then I spotted figures moving quietly between the red brick buildings. When they stepped into the light, I recognized the silver hair of the Dokkalfar. Definitely Night Elves. My heart quickened.

"They're here," I said.

Slowly, the Night Elves filed into the Common. My

stomach tightened. Though there were three hundred of them, the same number as in our cohort, there looked to be far fewer.

They looked small, weak. Easy to break. Emaciated, their arms were sinewy. They brandished a motley collection of swords and shields. Worse, while I was dressed in a full suit of plate armor, I didn't see so much as a single link of chainmail among them. They were woefully unprepared for the fight to come. Clearly, they'd agreed to this out of complete desperation. They were out here fighting for survival, sacrificing three hundred in an attempt to save the rest.

My stomach sank as they formed up into a loose line facing us. Fear coursed through my veins, as cold as the snow at my feet. If we were British soldiers, the Night Elves were the Minutemen. And, like the British soldiers at the first Battle of Lexington, I knew with gut-wrenching certainty I was about to participate in a bloody massacre.

I scanned the faces of the Night Elves. I couldn't see Ali anywhere, but presumably, she was among them. Once I found her, I would have to do everything in my power to protect her. I had to keep her alive.

Even if I hadn't seen her in my vision of the future, Wyrd had bound our souls, and I felt that more strongly than anything.

Again, I scanned the line of Night Elves. Worry snaked up my spine. She'd told me she'd received a mark. Where was she?

My muscles tensed as a shout rose from our ranks. King Gorm had begun to stride along the front of our line. Dressed in gold plate with an ivory cape slung over his shoulders, he looked every part the military commander. I wondered how many elves realized how nervous and fearful he actually was.

"Welcome to Midgard." The king's voice boomed over the

snowy field. As he paused to allow the sound of his voice to reverberate over the frozen ground, a figure stepped from the line of Night Elves.

Dressed in gray and holding only a small dagger, the Night Elf was wrinkled and stooped. I recognized her as Thyra, the oldest of the Shadow Lords.

"Thank you for calling for a Winnowing, King Gorm." Thyra spoke in a clear voice. "We look forward to fighting in this melee. May the blood spilled today bring glory to both our peop—"

"The sun has almost set," Gorm cut in. "Is everyone aware of the rules of the melee? No arrows. No wands. I have posted guards on the roof of the old carousel to watch the action." He paused to let the information sink in before he continued. "There are three hundred combatants on each side. No one leaves the field until half have fallen. Is that acceptable?"

A hundred yards away, I saw Thyra nod, glaring at him.

"Good," he shouted over the wind. He turned, pointing to the old carousel, to the High Elves crouched on its frozen roof. "In addition to being armed with stunning spells, I have tasked these elves to count the fallen. When the three hundredth elf falls, they will stop the fight. The side with the fewest deaths wins the trial."

Gorm was beginning to walk to the back of the line when Thyra spoke again. Her voice cut through the frozen air like a hot knife. "King Gorm, I have one question."

King Gorm spun on his heels. "What is it?"

"Respectfully, sir, who cut off your balls?"

A hush fell over the field as King Gorm's face turned a deep red.

"What is this impudence?" he bellowed.

"Why are you walking to the back of your soldiers?"

Thyra pointed her dagger at Gorm. "Only a coward refuses to lead his men into battle."

I did my best to suppress a smile. Thyra was goading Gorm, trying to provoke his temper. I wondered if this insight into his character had come from Ali.

Gorm's eyes blazed with anger, and his normally melodious voice cracked with rage. "Feral hag, you are going to die for those words."

He drew his sword and leveled it at the line of Night Elves.

"Kill them!" His voice boomed. "And bring me the bitch's head."

CHAPTER 11

ALI

Bo, the other Night Elves, and I were hidden in the snow along the edge of a frozen grove of maple trees. To our right was the carousel. Spread out in front of us was the line of High Elves facing off against the Night Elves. Snow whirled in the air, catching the last rays of the sun. A gentle hill sloped up to our left, toward the Citadel. I scanned the line for what must have been nearly the thousandth time.

I had bracers on my wrists and a leather cuirass protecting my chest. The light armor would give me a speed and agility advantage.

But where was Galin? If he was among the High Elves, I couldn't tell which one was him. They all looked identical in their armor, gleaming in the golden sunlight.

Fear gnawed at me. What if he hadn't come? What if he was too powerful to risk? I didn't think that was the case—he was their greatest fighter. But it was possible that I'd spent the last sixteen hours shivering in the cold snow for nothing.

I was here to kill him. This, without a doubt, was going to be my best chance. Had my plan failed?

I'd imagined this moment a hundred times while I was in

the mines. He was enormous, six foot five and built like a warrior—but I had stealth on my side. Whatever advantages Galin might have in strength I could easily counter with speed and agility.

It wasn't a guaranteed win. But I had a shot, and a shot was all I needed to redeem myself.

In the distance, King Gorm screamed at Thyra, something about "the bitch's head." He was so angry I could see his white cloak shaking from here. His words echoed, then faded into silence. The air fell still. For the briefest of moments, a hush fell over the battlefield. Only snowflakes moved, sparkling in the long rays of the setting sun, rosy in the light.

Then, with a howling battle cry, the High Elves charged.

A painter would call this time of day the golden hour, when the light glowed like honey. It glinted off the armor of the High Elves, off the steel blades of their swords, off the churning snow at their feet.

"Hold," I whispered under my breath to Bo and the other Night Elves hidden beside me. "Hold."

The High Elves sprinted, racing closer and closer to the Night Elves. All eyes were fixed on Thyra. She stood stiff as a statue, her arm held straight up, the tiny dagger glinting in her wizened fist.

The plan was simple. When Thyra lowered the blade, the Night Elves would raise their spears. Bo and I had spent the night hiding them in the snow, and they were ready to kill High Elves. If we got the timing just right, Gorm and the High Elves would be unable to stop in time. Their momentum would cause them to literally impale themselves.

The High Elves were halfway across the field now. A white miasma of snow billowed around them. A few more seconds and the trap would be set.

"Hold," I whispered.

Then, with a crack like a thunderclap, an inky circle appeared at the edge of the Common.

The High Elves slowed. I could see the confusion spreading through their ranks as the circle expanded, growing larger. Even from my distant vantage point, I knew what it was. A portal.

What in Hel was going on? Whatever it was, it had completely fucked up my concentration. And that was not ideal.

A figure charged from it. He had black hair, wore silver bracers on his arms, and was waving a flag above his head, shouting. Behind him, more figures emerged. All of them had hair as black as ravens' wings, eyes green as emeralds.

The Vanir. What the fuck were they doing here?

The High Elves slowed their charge, then stopped. Even Thyra turned to look. All eyes were on the new arrivals, probably wondering what was going on.

A new voice cut through the winter air: "We demand to participate in the Winnowing!" one of the Vanir shouted. He wore finer clothes, and a hawk was perched on his shoulder. If I had to guess, I would say he was their new leader, considering the Emperor was dead.

For a long beat, no one spoke.

"Who the Hel are you?" Gorm finally bellowed, breaking the silence.

"We are sons of Freyja, elves of golden plains and purple mountains. You may know us as the Vanir."

"You were not invited—"

"Do you deny the laws of Elfheim?" the Vanir leader interrupted. "Is it not true that any tribe declaring an ongoing conflict may participate, and select three hundred fighters? We have harbored resentments against the Night Elves and High Elves since Ragnarok. We demand a chance to prove ourselves, to conquer through a Winnowing."

Gorm stared at them. Even Thyra looked confused. Why would they want to be part of this? It made no sense.

"We only wish to add our blood to the battlefield," said the leader of the Vanir. "So that we may also have a chance at supremacy over our foes."

"No—" Gorm began, but the Vanir leader ignored him, turning instead to Thyra.

"Night Elves, do you recognize our right to fight in this melee?"

"Technically, yes," said Thyra slowly. "You are correct. Since the dawn of time, all tribes of elves have been allowed to fight in Winnowings."

"Then it is decided by a majority," the Vanir leader said. "As is our right and privilege, we will join this battle. We will spill our blood on this frozen land, help slay the weak and feeble."

Gorm took a hesitant step back, towards the line of High Elves.

By this point, the Vanir had formed into a third line, perpendicular to the lines of Night and High Elves. This was a battle formation that I hadn't anticipated, and that likely no one else had, since it made no fucking sense whatsoever.

I swallowed hard. Muscular and strong, the Vanir warriors wore silver bracers, had steel plates sewn into their shirts, and held curving sabers. They were ready for battle.

Their leader looked to the elves atop the roof of the carousel, then spoke in a booming voice. "The total is now nine hundred. Stop the melee when four hundred and fifty remain." Then, the Vanir leader drew his saber with a shout and charged forward. "Brothers, let us show them no mercy!"

CHAPTER 12

GALIN

My chest heaved. Sweat stung my eyes, and blood pounded in my ears. At the moment, it was hard to remember a time when this had sent a thrill through my body, when battle felt like it all had meaning. When death had served a greater purpose and the gods imbued us all with glory.

With my soul back, I felt the loss of the gods, a world devoid of meaning without them. When they'd died, I had, too. Having come into my living body once more, the loss was fresh to me now, a sharp blade in my heart.

With each movement on the battlefield, I felt that loss gnawing in my chest, eating at me. The only bright spark in this world of darkness was Ali.

I had no idea how long I'd been fighting, and I was only fighting defensively. I didn't want to kill Night Elves, just to stay alive and to protect Ali.

Still, my arms ached from slashing, stabbing, and parrying. I'd killed, and would continue to kill until either I fell or I found Ali. And yet, as much as I scanned the elves around me, I didn't see a single sign of her.

All around me, blades clashed, steel scraped against armor. Elves grunted with exhaustion and pain. The cries of the dying mixed with the shouts of the living. The mass of battling elves surged in random directions, driven only by each elf's desperate fight for survival.

As I stepped over a body, steel flashed in my peripheral vision, catching my attention just in time. I parried, my blade carving through the attacker's neck. Another one dead, and my sword gleamed scarlet.

Something slammed into my helmet, and my vision flashed white. I faltered. My visor was smashed, stuck, and I couldn't see. I couldn't see.

The fucking Helm of Awe didn't help the situation.

With a snarl, I ripped off my helmet. My blade dripped with fresh blood as I breathed in the frigid air. An elf nearby took a spear in the neck, and warm droplets sprayed the side of my face. All around me, elves fought, bled, and died. And I knew only one thing with certainty.

We were *losing*.

Without the gods, without purpose, perhaps I wasn't the secret weapon they'd imagined.

Five minutes earlier, the Vanir had slammed into our right flank. They were clearly more interested in killing us than in slaughtering the Night Elves. Now, we faced two enemies, not one.

Unencumbered by plate armor, the Vanir leapt and spun, dervishes with razor-sharp sabers. I'd seen five High Elves fall in the first ten seconds alone. I killed the Vanir one by one, whirling and cutting them down, but my heart wasn't in it. Not like it used to be.

And no one had anticipated the Night Elves' spears.

The other High Elves had slammed into them at a full sprint, and the spears had torn through our armor. I'd lost my cuirass, dented beyond repair. My armor had been damaged. Now, I fought bare-chested, wearing only pauldrons for protection.

Screaming, a Vanir charged me, black hair flying and emerald eyes bright with bloodlust. For the briefest second, I wondered if I'd met him in Vanaheim, but I didn't have time to think about it before he was upon me. His saber was a streak of silver slashing at my now uncovered head.

With the speed of a storm wind, I thrust my sword up, parrying. Hot sparks stung my face as our blades met, and I knocked him back. He twisted, trying to slash again, but I hacked downward. Fresh blood streaked the snow.

"Galin!"

I spun in the direction of my name.

Like a cursed apparition, Revna appeared beside me. Her hair was matted with blood, and like me, she'd lost her helmet. Unlike me, when her golden eyes locked on mine, her expression was one of pure ecstasy. Strange to think I'd once felt that battle lust. Now, it felt perverse.

"How many?" Her voice fluted melodiously, in awful juxtaposition to the carnage around us.

"What?" I whirled, cutting down another Vanir who charged for me.

Revna grinned excitedly. "I've killed eight, maybe more."

Out of the fray, a Night Elf lunged with a spear. I chopped the weapon away. "Haven't been counting," I replied breathlessly. "Where's Gorm? Sune?"

But she was already gone, back into the swirling maelstrom of blood and blades. I was on my own again. Free for a moment.

I scanned the battle around me. Elves were fighting. Shouting. Screaming. Dying.

The Vanir were advancing. The Night Elves stabbed the fallen with their daggers and pressed in upon us. The battle was turning against us, but I didn't care. Because all I wanted was to make sure Ali was safe. I scanned the battlefield for her, trying to see her beautiful face through the haze of blood and steel.

Then, I smelled it. It was a scent—*her* scent--jasmine. Ali. I felt her presence, her soul near mine.

Acting only on instinct, I whirled. From the trees behind me, a group of Night Elves charged. My eyes locked on my soulmate. With her silver hair flowing behind her, Skalei tight in her fist, and her eyes blazing with rage, she looked like a goddess of war. My heart leapt. Fatigue, exhaustion, and fear evaporated, replaced by relief. She was alive. This time I wasn't going to let her get away.

Her eyes fixed on mine, her face a mask of pure, unadulterated rage.

My heart skipped a beat.

Ali was coming for me, and it looked like she wanted me dead.

I charged toward her.

CHAPTER 13

ALI

I caught a glimpse of the most heartbreakingly beautiful face I'd ever seen, and that was enough. Every fiber of my being said I'd found Galin. I felt like ice was shattering in my heart, but I would end him.

Calling Skalei and drawing my sword, I raced down the hill toward the battle at a dead-out sprint.

I bounded fast over the snow like a skipping stone, heading towards him. A Vanir swung a saber at me, but I easily dodged the blade and, with a spin, slashed my sword across his throat. Without missing a beat, I pushed forward. The trick was to never stop. Never give the enemy a chance to regroup.

Another Vanir warrior spotted me and lunged, screaming. His blade flashed, lethally sharp. I ducked. Rolled. Stabbed upwards. With a soft *thunk*, I introduced him to Skalei. He grunted once, then fell.

On my feet again, my head swiveled. I'd lost sight of Galin.

I sniffed the air and caught his scent of wood smoke and sage, distinct from all the others. That was when I saw him again, hacking through the elves around him, a maelstrom of death. His golden hair flew out behind him, his sword flashing in the night, red with blood. Unstoppable, he literally carved a path to me.

I gripped my sword, my dagger. Which one to use?

He was ten feet from me now, eyes locked on mine. I dropped my sword and leapt towards him, and his mouth opened, expression startled.

I was an eagle diving for the kill. Skalei, my sharpest talon, aimed straight for his heart.

Time slowed.

I'd spent hours shoveling rock, eating gruel, envisioning the sequence of events—I'd worked through all the scenarios. Every movement of my body. Each breath of my lungs. The clenching and unclenching of my muscles.

For some reason, his chest was uncovered. Just shoulder pauldrons and bare flesh. His runic tattoos glowed on his skin, unearthly in the twilight. Easy to spot—he would be easier to kill than I'd hoped.

I aimed for the gap between the third and fourth ribs. I imagined the sound of my blade punching into his body. The look in his eyes when he realized that his betrayal had a terrible consequence.

But *this* was no dream. This was really, actually happening. At last, vengeance was mine for the taking.

Like a striking viper, I flew at him. Skalei was an unstoppable blur aimed straight at his heart.

My forearm flexed, ready to drive the dagger home—

His sword flashed like a lightning bolt, right into Skalei's blade. The power of the strike raced up my arm like I'd just punched a brick wall, and Skalei flew away.

I hit the ground with a shoulder roll. The Sword of the Gods clearly deserved his nickname.

"Skalei." She came to me. On my feet, I spun to face Galin.

He pointed his sword at me, expression ferocious. "This is very much not the reunion I'd imagined."

I ignored him, charging forward. This time, I held Skalei close.

He raised his sword but seemed to hesitate. One more step, and I slashed up.

A normal dagger wouldn't stand a chance against a sword, but Skalei wasn't normal. She bit into the steel of Galin's sword, and I twisted hard, throwing all my weight into her. With a sharp crack, Galin's sword snapped.

That elicited an animal growl from him, and as I lunged for him again, blade ready, he blocked me with a forearm across my chest. His pale eyes gleamed, fierce and lethal.

The force of his blow knocked me flat on my ass, breathless. Gods, he was strong. Unreasonably strong, and he'd slammed the wind right out of me. Pain shot through my ribs.

My simmering rage gave me new strength, though, and I scissored my legs, taking his feet out from under him. It was like kicking a brick fucking wall, but it worked, and the giant of an elf fell backward in the snow.

"Skalei," I whispered, leaping up.

I was on him in moments, legs straddling his waist, catching my breath. I brought my dagger up—

Something stopped me. Was it that little smile on his lips? Why was he smiling?

"This is more like the reunion I'd imagined," he purred.

I started to bring down the dagger again, but he caught my wrist and squeezed—*hard.* Hard enough I thought he could break it.

Frustration bloomed in me, as well as a fear that I couldn't actually win this fight. The feeling grew even more when he threw me off him, making me roll in the snow.

Why had I hesitated?

"Skalei!"

I ran for him again, and he for me. He slammed into me, knocking me backward into an old oak frozen in the middle of the battlefield. His grip on my wrists was crushing, his expression stunned.

"I'm beginning to think you really mean to kill me," he said breathlessly.

"Oh, I do."

"And I'm starting to find your knife irritating."

I headbutted him hard, my skull connecting with his nose. When he stumbled back from me, I lunged again, aiming Skalei straight for his heart. He moved so fast, though, that it was nearly impossible to catch him.

Gods, he was quicker than I'd anticipated. He was like smoke on the wind, elusive.

My momentum began to carry me past him, so I planted my leading foot. Spraying snow around me, I turned back—but too slowly. One of his powerful hands latched around my wrist like a manacle, clutching it hard.

I looked up into his stupidly beautiful face, my vision clouding with rage.

"Why do I feel like you're actually trying to kill me?" he said, leaning in. I could feel his breath hot on my cheek. His golden eyes seeming to pierce my soul, searing right into me.

They made me feel something I didn't want to feel, a tightening in my heart. I gritted my teeth, trying to ignore that godlike face, the chiseled cheekbones.

I'd come for death, not to admire a pretty face. But clearly, in my weakened state, I was outmatched. The Sword of the Gods was strong and well-fed, and I would have to fight dirty. Trick him.

"Fine," I whispered.

Pretending to give up, I dropped Skalei. I watched as relief washed over Galin's face, his brows knitting earnestly as he began to pull me closer, drawing me into his intoxicating embrace.

He wouldn't charm me this time. Before the blade had a chance to hit the ground, I recalled her to my free hand. "Skalei."

Then, I swung hard, driving the blade at his stomach.

But he grabbed my wrists, then twisted me around so that he was behind me with my arms in front. I recalled Skalei, but he had full control of my hands.

His bare chest pressed against my back, his strong arms like steel around me. He was a vice of muscle. "If this is really how you want to spend our time together," he murmured, "I suppose I won't object. Maybe you can help me regain my lost love for violence. It's just that I'd prefer we fight *other* people, if you don't mind."

I felt his muscles flexing around me, and at that moment, I truly regretted his betrayal and that he was my worst enemy. I wished it had been someone revolting.

I bucked backward, shoving my ass into him. He slipped in the snow, off balance, and that was enough to free me. I whirled and kicked him hard in the solar plexus.

As he doubled over, finally, I pressed Skalei upward against the skin of his throat.

"On your knees," I gasped.

Galin obeyed, his eyes fixed on mine. He genuinely looked perplexed. Did he think I wouldn't come for him?

"You really think I wouldn't kill you after what you did?" I said, my voice just loud enough to be heard over the battle. Skalei was ready, sharp as she would ever be. It was finally time for vengeance. "This is for my mother, my father, and all the thousands of Night Elves who've died in darkness because of you. This is for the letter you wrote."

With a jerk, I drew the blade along his jugular.

Only ... I didn't.

His gaze was pulling me to pieces, like he was reading my darkest nightmares, my wildest dreams. My hand went still, and as I stared into his eyes, a warming light seemed to surround me. The air was filled with the scents of flowers and songs of bluebirds. I felt weightless, like a dandelion seed on a summer breeze. My fingers unclenched, and I dropped Skalei.

Was he using magic? I slammed my fist into his jaw, the force so strong I felt like I broke my knuckles. At least I'd landed a fucking punch.

But he hardly flinched. Instead, he rose to his full height, towering over me once more. He brushed my hair away from my ear, then leaned in, whispering, "You cannot truly hurt me."

This was unthinkable, unimaginable. I was supposed to be avenging the Night Elves. This was what I lived for. There was only one possible explanation: he'd enchanted me.

"Spells are not allowed," I snarled.

"This isn't a spell. Your soul is entwined with mine. The Norns have threaded our fates together."

Liar. I hated him more than he could possibly imagine. "I'm going to kill you."

"You can't. This is fate, Ali—Wyrd. Our souls are bound for eternity."

My heart went still, and I felt my chest hollowing out. "What are you talking about? You *have* to die. The Dokkalfar have suffered a thousand years because of you. I swore to Thyra I would kill you, to my parents before they died. And I hardly feel any loyalty to you after what you did."

Despite the snow, the air around us smelled like summertime: fresh grass and lilacs. Not that I cared. And, I certainly wasn't giving up.

Snarling, I ran for him, leaping into the air like a wild beast. Galin caught me mid-air, then slammed me against the tree again. My legs were wrapped tight around his waist as he pressed me against the icy bark. He'd knocked the wind out of me, but he'd slid his hands behind me just in time to cushion the blow. He'd managed to cup my head, wrap his arms around my back so I wasn't hurt. Why couldn't he just fight properly?

"Skalei," I whispered.

But before I could cut his throat, he gripped my wrist, pressing it against the tree so I couldn't use Skalei against him.

"You're not faking this fight," He leaned down, his mouth just above mine. "Like I said before, this must look like a battle. I won't hurt you. But you are trying to kill me."

"I *was* actually fighting," I whispered. "Not pretending."

There it was—that flash of confusion. No, hurt.

But as he looked at me, I could feel a strange, forbidden warmth tingling over my skin at every point where our bodies made contact. His muscled chest pressed against me, his hand against my throat, his hips between my legs. My pulse started racing.

He slid his thumb down just a little, I felt an illicit, molten heat sliding into my belly. His mouth hovered over my neck, his breath warming my throat. "Our souls are conjoined," he purred. "Bound to one another for eternity. *We* are the only thing that matters. You and me. It is the only meaning that exists for me now." He lifted his face to mine, and I read a look of pure, carnal longing in his eyes.

It was insanity. Absolute insanity.

And yet somehow, the words rang true in the darkest recesses of my mind.

"Just because we traveled to Hel and back doesn't mean you know anything about me," I protested.

"Our souls must be together. Wyrd demands it. We have no choice. When I am king, you will be my queen. Or we will run away. I really don't care. I only know I want you by my side, and you are trying to murder me."

"Are you insane? If this is true, why did you write that letter?" It was hard for me to think clearly with his mouth hovering so close, and worst of all, I found my neck arching, as if I was *purposefully* making myself more vulnerable to him.

This had to be magic.

"What are you talking about?" he murmured, and the deep timber of his voice skittered over my skin. "What letter?"

But a new voice interrupted us now. "Ali!"

I glimpsed Bo over Galin's shoulder. Had he witnessed us … well, I wasn't entirely sure what we had been doing, but it wasn't quite fighting.

And worse, Bo was probably spying on me for Thyra to see if I was still working with Galin. I pulled Galin's hands from me, unclasped my legs, and wriggled out of his grasp.

Pushing past the enormous High Elf, I could finally see Bo. He stood staring at us, his eyes gleaming, and I watched as his fingers tightened on his sword. "Get away from him, Ali."

I could tell from the intensity of his gaze that he had recognized Galin. A moment later, he started sprinting for him, blade raised.

Galin no longer had a sword, and for some reason, he opened his arms, like he was welcoming the charging Night Elf.

What is he doing?

Just as I had done, Bo lunged at full speed, his sword carving a furious arc in the air, silver hair streaking behind him. I didn't want to watch Galin die, but it had to happen. First Galin, then the other royals.

I stepped back, waiting for the blood to flow. For Galin to fall.

But instead, Bo stiffened, then fell to the blood-soaked snow.

A moment after he hit the ground, the dolorous toll of a bell exploded across the battlefield, filling my ears and making my head ache. My heart dropped into my stomach as I watched the remaining warriors charging off the Common.

Galin turned to me, fury burning in his eyes. "Seems that the quota's been reached. The melee is over. Thanks for the help, Ali."

I stared at him, stunned. What did this mean about our souls being entwined? Maybe I felt it somewhere in the dark hollows of my thoughts, but….

Was this some sorcerer bullshit he was pulling? It was hard to think clearly when he was anywhere near me.

Whatever the case, I couldn't let anyone see me speaking to him. They already had me pegged as a traitor.

His jaw was now set tight, and he stalked closer to me, cutting me a sharp look. "You would have let him kill me, wouldn't you? And you were really trying to end my life?" Moments ago, he'd been murmuring that we were meant to be. Now, his voice sounded cold as ice.

I had so many questions to ask, but with the melee over anyone could be watching. I simply said, "That's what I came here to do. Avenge my parents and my tribe. I will defeat the High Elves. You first, then the rest of your rancid family."

He looked at me, searching my face for a long moment. Then, he stalked away, into the center of the battlefield, the muscles of his back coiled and angry.

For some insane reason, watching him walk away from me, I felt glass shattering in my heart.

CHAPTER 14

GALIN

Darkness clouded my mind. The gods were dead, Ali hated me, and nothing meant anything anymore.

Perhaps when she had come to my room, she'd simply been using me for information, but she'd never planned to return to me.

I surveyed the carnage around me.

After nearly twelve hundred years, the Common had finally become a battlefield. What had earlier in the day been white snow was now soaked and splattered with crimson, a mottled patchwork of death and slaughter.

Strewn all over the snow, like leaves after a windstorm, were the bodies of elves. Dead and dying, they lay in groups. Black, blond, and silver hair mingled for the first time in more than a thousand years.

I stalked through the center of the carnage, blood-smeared and exhausted. Around me, elves were calling out, some in pain, some with grief. Small groups of still-upright elves moved over the muddy ground—the grim process of helping the wounded and collecting the dead was beginning, but I hardly noticed. My thoughts were fixed on Ali.

She truly hated me still, didn't she? She had meant to let me die. Perhaps she wasn't my destiny, then, even if our souls were bound. Perhaps fate was punishing me.

When I turned back to look at her, I found her kneeling by the elf who'd tried to kill me, the lanky one who'd been slammed with a stunning spell for attacking after the melee was over.

As our eyes met, she gave me a final, hard look. There was nothing but pure hatred and sorrow in her gaze.

I turned away from her, and as I did, my sister sidled up next to me. Gore smeared her golden armor and matted her hair, but she looked happy.

"Are you injured?" I asked.

Revna laughed as though it was a complete impossibility. "Do I look like I'm in pain, dearest brother?"

"Your cheek is bleeding."

"Oh, this?" she said, touching a finger to the blood. "It's not mine. This is the blood of our enemies. I slew at least twenty." She licked one of her blood-soaked fingers. "You must remember the taste of victory?"

"Where's Sune?"

"I don't know."

She turned, her eyes narrowing, and I followed her gaze to Ali. Revna's grin curdled my stomach as she pivoted, striding right over to Ali. She pointed at her.

"You there, night wretch. Look at me."

Ali rose slowly, and I heard Revna's tinkling laughter.

"I thought it was you, cave-swine. How's your finger?"

"This one?" Ali flipped up her middle finger. "It's fine."

Revna laughed. "Aren't you clever? Now I see why Galin took you with him into the Well, even if you have a mutilated hand."

Ali looked right at me, eyes like flecks of ice. "Your entire family is amazingly vile."

Not going to argue with that.

"And we remain enemies," she added.

I turned, stalking away.

* * *

Next to me, Revna walked calmly among the bodies. In her gore-smeared armor, with her sword still dripping with blood, she looked like a valkyrie choosing which among the slain would rise and go to the gods' halls. Except the valkyries had honor.

I shuddered as reality sunk in. This was the future, the place Wyrd was currently leading us. If Gorm and Revna continued to rule, there would only be more battles, more massacres. Death and destruction were the High Elves' identity.

"Do you know how many we lost?" I asked.

"Our side? One hundred and seventy-eight." Revna nodded grimly. "One hundred and twenty-two High Elves, one hundred and sixty-one Night Elves, and one hundred and sixty-seven Vanir remain."

I'd come here wanting to take Ali away from all this, but now that seemed completely unlikely. At least the Night Elves were surviving.

"Did you know it was possible to kill an elf simply by stabbing them in the balls?" said Revna. "Wait here."

She ran ahead of me. She stopped by a fallen soldier, a Night Elf. The elf moved, seeming to ask for help, but Revna knelt, and I saw a blade flash in her hand. The elf fell back to the snow.

I snarled, my blood running cold. "That was against the rules of the Winnowing."

She turned to look at me, glee dancing in her eyes. "Haven't you heard? Nothing matters except for winning. And I like it that way."

I leaned close so no one could hear me speak. "Your lack of honor is an embarrassment."

In a flash, Revna had her dagger at my throat. "But you wouldn't turn me in, would you, brother?"

I reached for her wrist, but before I could pull her hand away, the Helm of Awe hummed, and a blazing gout of magic hit me like a sledgehammer between my eyes. Pain split my mind. Even with the helm weakened, I felt like it was ripping my skull open. I clutched my head.

"You see?" she trilled. "You cannot hurt your own flesh and blood. Do not tell me what I can and cannot do."

I curled my lip, a low growl in my throat. I would kill her when I killed Gorm.

* * *

AT THE TOP of the hill was an ancient carousel buried under the snow. It looked a bit like an enormous frosted cake, though the effect was disturbed by the weathered faces of wooden horses poking out from under the drifts.

In front, I found Gorm stomping around in the snow, Sune next to him. The king's face was beet-red with anger.

"What in the darkest Hel happened? We were gods-damned slaughtered out there." He glared at me. "Galin! How did you not foresee this?"

I shrugged. "I'm not omniscient."

The king stalked towards me, his sword gripped tightly in his hand. "Who in Hel were those saber wielding elves?"

"As they said when they arrived, they're the Vanir."

He kicked a snow drift. Spittle flew from his mouth. "Loki's blood! I want to destroy them."

I'd never seen Gorm quite like this. Nearly unhinged. Raging. He paced back and forth before the carousel like a caged lion. It delighted me.

"What are we going to do?" He swung his sword, carving it through the head of a wooden carousel horse. Suddenly, he spun, pointing the sword at my bare chest. "I asked you a question."

I flashed him a smile. "You are the king. Surely, in your infinite wisdom, you foresaw this possibility and have already devised a plan."

With the back of my hand, I slapped his sword away, and fear flickered in his eyes. I didn't think I would have been able to do that before I'd weakened the helm.

He turned from me, ranting again, shaking the sword with frustration. "This was our chance. We designed the agreement with the Night Elves so that we would have the advantage. Now, we are completely out of options."

Now *this* was interesting. "What do you mean advantage? What did you agree upon?"

He swung his sword again, decapitating another horse. Splinters of wood flew into the air. "The contract states that Night Elves get to choose the second battle—the next contest. It could be anything. We were supposed to have an overwhelming lead after this. They are going to pick something that plays to their strengths."

It took every ounce of my willpower not to smile.

The Night Elves were succeeding.

CHAPTER 15

ALI

I picked Skalei from the snow, cold and slick with blood. I clutched her to my chest like a child might hold a teddy bear.

Dazed, I staggered through the snow, pacing back and forth near Bo.

I was still trying to take in what Galin had said. Soul mates. None of this fit with my training.

My training was unequivocal. Suppress any sorrow, smother your sadness. Only hatred was acceptable. Become the North Star; avenge your people. Bring down the wall with his death. Channel rage, feed on it, bathe in it, use its power to guide your hand.

And he'd betrayed me, hadn't he? I still didn't understand why he'd wanted me sent to the mines. Why screw me over one moment and try to whisper sweet nothings in my ear the next? Was he simply messing with my mind for kicks? It was the sort of thing his warped sister would do.

I hate him. I hate him. I hate him.

For a moment, the mantra worked. Until it didn't.

I was staggering now, like I'd been hit in the head.

I clutched Skalei tighter. She'd been through it all. Minutes ago, she'd cut down a Vanir out for my blood, and in the past few months, she'd killed a nokk, slew the Emperor of the Vanir, and carved a hole in Nidhogg's gut. I'd lost track of how many times she'd stabbed Galin when he'd been a lich.

I needed to focus and stop feeling sorry for myself. I drew the pad of my thumb along Skalei's edge until fresh blood dripped on the snow. The burst of pain sharpened my mind.

I stared at Skalei. Razor-sharp and unflinching. With this little dagger, one way or another, I was going to lead my people to freedom. Today, I may have failed as an assassin, but I wouldn't give up.

I turned back to look at Bo. Corpse-stiff, he lay flat, up to his ears in mud. Only his eyes moved, staring at me.

I knelt again. "Are you okay?"

Bo moaned. A strange gurgling sound.

"You'll recover." I sat back on my heels. What was I going to do with him? Thyra had told everyone to spy on me. He was supposed to report back if he saw me do anything treasonous. And I wasn't exactly sure what it had looked like when Galin pinned me up against the tree, but it clearly hadn't looked like me killing him.

If the Shadow Lords thought I'd been consorting with Galin, they wouldn't throw me back into the mines. No, Thyra would take my head off right here in the Common.

My gripped tightened on Skalei's hilt.

I leaned close. Anyone watching would only see that Bo was injured and that I was tending to him. I pressed Skalei's cool steel to his neck—not hard enough to cut the skin, but an obvious threat. His eyes widened.

Keeping the blade to his jugular, I held a finger to my lips.

He stared at me, his eyes filled with terror.

"Did you see anything you feel the need to report to Thyra?"

He didn't speak, but the rapid dilation of his pupils told me all I needed to know.

"Well, then, here's what's going to happen," I said in a sharp whisper. "You're not going to tell anyone what you saw, and I'm not going to kill you. Okay?"

Bo's response was an unintelligible gurgle.

"Move your eyes back and forth if you agree."

Bo's eyes darted like he was reading the hottest scene in a romance novel.

"Good. Now, don't forget that later, when my knife isn't at your throat. It doesn't mean it couldn't be again. Understood?" I paused and sighed. "I'm still on your side. Galin was simply using some kind of magic on me. That's all. But I will fight for the Night Elves until my last dying breath, and that is the truth."

Bo's eyes shifted again.

"All right. Now that we have an agreement, I'm going to get someone to help you with this paralysis spell."

I stood and began making my way toward a large group of Night Elves. The Shadow Lords stood in the front. As I walked toward them, my thoughts returned to Galin. During the fight, I hadn't thought to get any answers out of him, like what the fuck had motivated him to send that letter.

And I had to wonder if what he'd said was true. Had the Norns bound our souls together with fate?

All I knew was that Galin now consumed every one of my thoughts—every heartbeat, every breath of air—and I needed to burn him out of my mind.

CHAPTER 16

ALI

It seemed impossible, but after a bloody battle, we were now waiting for the High Elves to serve *us* dinner.

After the battle, things had started moving quickly. King Gorm had led us through the streets of Boston in a sort of grand parade. High Elves had lined the streets, morosely "cheering" and throwing snow into the air like confetti, their expressions murderous.

Then, the High Elves had brought us to the Citadel as guests of honor. Once inside, we'd been given a few hours to bathe and put on fresh clothes. After that, we had been led to an enormous mead hall.

The Citadel kitchens must have been working overtime, because when we arrived, the mead hall was filled with tables, enough to seat every elf in the Winnowing, including the Vanir. Ivory tablecloths, gilded place settings, and crystal wine glasses were laid out in neat rows. Above us, candles flickered in gilded chandeliers.

We were arranged by tribe in three long rows—the High Elves in the middle and the Vanir and Night Elves on either side. At one end of the hall was a low stage. I sat with the Night Elf leadership just in front, squeezed between Thyra and Ilvis. I would have liked to think this was an honor, but I suspected instead that they were keeping a close eye on me.

I didn't see any signs of Gorm or the rest of the High Elf royalty. Probably for the best. I wasn't sure what I would do if I had to eat dinner ten feet from Galin.

"Ali, are you alright?" Thyra asked.

"I'm fine," I said. "Just really tired."

That much was true. I was exhausted. Not only had I fought in a battle, I'd been up for nearly twenty-four hours, much of it spent shivering in the snow. My body ached.

Thyra touched my shoulder gently. "You did well out there."

I looked down at my empty plate. The Shadow Lord was kinder than I'd expected. She wouldn't be kind if she knew I'd had a chance to kill Galin and thrown it away. I felt like I'd thrown something else away, too, but I couldn't quite piece my feelings together into anything coherent.

I wanted to change the subject. "How long do you suppose it will be before they feed us?"

The faintest hint of a smile wrinkled the Shadow Lord's face. "Who knows? I don't think the High Elves expected this many guests."

"And they will house us?"

"Yes, the contract states that the High Elves are to house and feed all participating elves until the Winnowing is complete."

I let out a low whistle. "Fancy."

Last time I'd visited the Citadel, King Gorm had tried to have me killed, and I'd nearly been thrown down the Well of Wyrd. Now, I was about to be served a feast in their main hall as a guest of honor.

"Excuse me?" A golden-haired elf appeared between us.

Dressed in a black and white servant's outfit, she held a large pitcher of golden liquid. "Shall I fill your cup?"

Thyra shook her head.

"And you, miss?" she asked me. "Would you care for some mead?"

After today's events, there was no way I was going to say no to free booze. "Hel yes. Please."

The server filled my glass with the golden liquid. It smelled herbal and faintly sweet, and I eagerly took a sip. Crisp and dry, with only the faintest taste of honey. *Gods, I could get used to this. We don't have this sort of thing underground.*

When a trumpet suddenly sounded, I jumped, nearly spilling the mead across my plate. Seemed I was still a little tense from the battle.

A herald dressed in golden stockings, a cream doublet, and a gold embroidered coat stood in the center of the stage. He pressed a calf's horn to his lips and blew a long note until the hall was silent, then he spoke. "Announcing his Royal Majesty, Ruler of Midgard, Leader of the High Elves, King Gorm, accompanied by his family: Princes Galin and Sune, and lovely Princess Revna."

So much for a Galin-free dinner.

From a side door, King Gorm appeared and strode onto the stage, chest puffed. He wore gold velvet and a white fur mantle, which certainly lent him a regal appearance. Behind him followed Revna, Sune, and Galin. Like their father, Revna and Sune wore golden outfits.

Galin, however, wore a tailored indigo suit, so dark it might have been black. Atop his head rested the Helm of Awe.

"Thank you all for coming," said King Gorm. His voice seemed strained, not the usual bold, melodious tones he'd used when I'd seen him previously.

I could guess why. This was supposed to be his time to

gloat. If the melee had gone as he'd intended, there would only have been a few dozen Night Elves left alive. In that scenario, he'd have played the part of a benevolent ruler generously serving a huge feast to his captives, using the dinner to demoralize us with a grand show of the High Elves' wealth. Reminding us that we'd soon die.

Instead, the High Elves had been caught off guard and soundly beaten. He'd had to scramble to find room for all of us.

Gorm took a seat in the center of the table, with Revna and Sune on one side and Galin on the other. Galin sipped his mead, and it seemed he had no interest whatsoever in looking in my direction.

The servers began to hurry around, placing steaming trays of venison, salmon, and turkey on the tables. My stomach growled when they brought out the side dishes. Platters of potatoes slathered in butter, bowls full of asparagus and broccoli, and great boules of fresh bread.

I filled my plate, then turned to Thyra. "So, what's the plan now that the Vanir have joined in?"

"The Winnowing is always the same, each tribe chooses a contest."

"So"—I did some quick math in my head—"we stop when there are only one hundred and thirteen elves left."

"Correct."

"Is it true that you've done this before?"

Thyra nodded. "Before Ragnarok, the High Elves and Night Elves fought in a Winnowing to end centuries of battle."

"What happened then?"

"Lots of elves died, but it ended in a truce. Until Ragnarok, when they defeated us completely," said Thyra in an unusually quiet voice. I got the impression she didn't enjoy this topic of conversation. She speared a piece of salmon and popped it in her mouth, chewing thoughtfully. "But now, we feast, and in the next round, we choose the contest."

That was good news. "Have you decided what it will be?"

"No, not yet."

But an idea was starting to form in my mind, a seedling of a plan blooming larger.

CHAPTER 17

GALIN

Next to me, my father cut into his turkey, alternating his ravenous eating with gulps of mead. Strange. A normal man wouldn't have an appetite after what had happened. He'd been ranting on the battlefield, but now that there was a plate of food in front of him, all was forgotten. And that made me wonder what the fuck he was up to.

Worry quelled my appetite. Ali was less than twenty feet away, sitting between a pair of Shadow Lords. She looked thinner than when I'd last seen her, starving as she wolfed down her meal.

And worst of all, as soon as Gorm recognized her, he would know the truth. She was a high value target, one he never should have given up. And that would provoke his rage, directed at me.

I'd tried to keep Gorm away from the feast. I'd told him that he would look weak parading the royal family across the stage, especially after we'd just come in last place. But his desire for adulation was too much, and he'd insisted on making an appearance.

I needed a plan. The reality was that Gorm *was* going to find out who Ali was. Either he'd recognize her himself, or Revna would tell him. Even though Ali wanted to kill me, I would find a way to warn her. Her life was in grave danger, and whether she loathed me or not, I wanted her alive.

And most of all, I needed to redouble my efforts to get the helm off my head. The magic was weaker, but I needed to be completely free of the infernal crown.

I surveyed the mead hall, taking in the scene.

The Vanir leader sat at the head of his table, the hawk I'd seen at the battle still perched on his shoulder. He caught my eye, then tossed a piece of meat to the bird. As the creature devoured it in messy bites, its master stared me down like he wanted to murder me.

Perhaps he and Ali could bond over that particular fantasy.

"Galin," said my father suddenly. When I turned to look at him, I saw a little flash of apprehension in his eyes. "I want you to stay after the meal. I'm taking the leaders of the Vanir and Night Elves on a little after-dinner outing. But perhaps you could act as host as well."

"I suppose." Inwardly, I was relieved. I'd have a chance to warn Ali.

Gorm returned to his plate of turkey and mashed potatoes.

Later, when the servers cleared our plates, the king rose from his seat and spread his arms.

"Thank you all for coming to dinner." He pointed to a group of guards dressed in gold embroidered uniforms. "These elves will lead you to your rooms." As the Night Elf leaders and Vanir began to stand, he spoke more softly, in his usual melodious tones, "Leaders of your tribes, please stay. I have some evening entertainment planned, and we have much to discuss. Please, join me on the dais."

While the elves continued to file out, Ali started to make her way to the dais, flanked by two Shadow Lords. I had the impression they were guarding her somehow. Behind them trailed the Vanir leader.

And then it was just us—the High Elf leadership and a handful of our greatest enemies. Including my mate.

Ali shot me a sharp look, and I tore my eyes away from her.

"Thyra," said King Gorm in his deep baritone. "Let me congratulate you on your success today. One hundred sixty-one of your elves survived. That is quite the feat."

Thyra's expression remained unchanged. "Maybe, but I lost one hundred and thirty-nine of my elves."

Gorm waved away her worries. "Come, come. It is a great honor to give your life in battle. Surely, your elves ascended to Valhalla. Tonight, they are drinking Heidrun's mead and singing with the valkyries." He was just lifting his glass, when he suddenly stiffened, nearly spilling his mead. "What are *you* doing here?"

I followed his gaze to Ali. Tonight, she looked every bit the Night Elf assassin. Tight leather pants and shirt, hair pulled up, a shadow dagger at her hip. My pulse raced at the sight of her. And I felt my heart breaking, too.

"Oh, hello again." She held out her hand. "I don't believe we were ever properly introduced. Every time we met before, you seemed rather intent on throwing me into your well. I'm Astrid, daughter of Volundar, Chief Assassin of the Shadow Lords."

For an instant, Gorm's gaze flicked to me. It was only a second, but the expression was easy enough to read. Pure fury.

He started to introduce Revna. Presumably, he thought she would be able to intimidate Ali. He was wrong.

"Oh, we've already met," Ali cooed, her eyes glacial.

"Shame we didn't meet during the melee. There's something I meant to pay back." She lifted her hand, displaying the nub where Revna had severed her ring finger.

For the first time in my very long life, I saw my sister completely on her heels. "Oh, yes," she stammered. "Well, I will try to make sure that doesn't happen."

"Enough pleasantries," said Thyra suddenly. She nodded at the Vanir leader. "Now, I don't believe we have been introduced."

He was tall, with the typical Vanir appearance: ebony hair, green eyes, and bronzed skin. He wore a black vest that exposed thick, muscular arms. His trousers appeared to be made of buckskin. He had a rough look, as if he was about to go bear hunting.

He bowed deeply, then spoke. "I'm Swegde, Regent to the Empire of the Vanir."

Thyra frowned. "Regent? I thought the Vanir were led by an emperor?"

Swegde bowed his head solemnly. "Our Emperor died unexpectedly a few weeks ago." He shot a sharp look at Ali, and a heavy silence fell over us. Bit awkward, given that the Emperor's assassin was right here.

"Well, now that everyone is properly acquainted," King Gorm interrupted, "let us chat over drinks." He walked to the entrance of the mead hall, saying, "This way," over his shoulder.

He was taking us out to the courtyard? Odd. He had something planned.

When we reached the arched doorway to the Citadel, I paused. Normally, exiting the Citadel would cause the Helm of Awe to shock me. My mind spun as I tried to piece together what Gorm's play was.

In the center of the courtyard stood a large structure that I recognized as the royal barge. Constructed from mahogany and large glass windows on all sides, it looked a bit like a very large 19th century carriage. Unlike the stately carriages of the Victorian Era, however, gold gleamed on every surface.

Odd to see it resting on the frozen courtyard stones. Before Ragnarok, Gorm had spent hours floating on the lakes of Elfheim on the barge, drinking copious amounts of mead.

Swegde's dark hair caught in the icy wind as he turned toward the king. "What is this contraption?"

Gorm held out his arms, smiling. "This is the royal barge."

"But there is no water," replied Swegde. "What does it float on?"

"Come aboard and all will be revealed."

A guard opened a pair of gilded doors in the side of the barge. As we lined up, I noticed Ali seemed to be doing her best to stay as far away from me as possible. The relationship between us, at this point, seemed as frozen as the world around us. I tried desperately to put her out of my mind as I boarded the barge behind the king.

I couldn't focus on Ali when I needed to stay alert, to anticipate Gorm's actions. If he tried to hurt those around me, I would cut him to ribbons even if the helm fried my mind.

As I stepped inside, I felt a slight wave of disgust. The last time I'd been inside the barge had been over a thousand years ago, and I'd forgotten how ostentatious it was. Virtually everything was gilded, from the frames of the windows to the bar; even the seat cushions were stitched with shining golden threads.

King Gorm led us out a door and onto a small exterior platform with a golden railing.

A High Elf dressed in a captain's uniform followed after us. "Where to, Your Majesty?"

Gorm lifted his hands expansively. "Let's show them the city."

The captain whistled sharply, the sound echoing in the otherwise empty courtyard. Then, a massive flock of giant moths swooped down from the sky. They were so large and numerous they blotted out the stars, and the beating of their wings stirred the frigid air, blowing up clouds of snow from the ground.

From each moth hung a thin golden cord. As they circled above us, more High Elves climbed onto the roof of the barge. Dressed in blue uniforms, they began to tie the cords to a large brass ring in the center of the barge's roof.

The captain climbed into a small seat on the roof. "Ready, men?" he shouted. "Aloft!"

The barge lifted smoothly into the air, and the wind rushed over us as we rose. In moments, we were flying above the Citadel. A few snowflakes fell from the night sky, and the frozen city of Boston spread out below us. Twinkling lights nestled within a vast expanse of darkness. As the barge climbed higher, the breeze stiffened, and the snow grew heavier.

In her black leather, Ali looked tense, her fingers always twitching as if she planned to call her dagger.

She had good reason to be tense.

"Let us go back inside," Gorm called above the wind.

Back in the cabin, a veritable smorgasbord of pastries had been arranged on tables, along with great steaming carafes of hot chocolate and coffee. Red velvet sofas had been pulled up around a gilded coffee table.

"Make yourselves comfortable," said Gorm.

I kept standing, my mind always churning, strategizing how I'd make my move if I needed to.

"We have much to discuss," said Gorm. "I thought the next contest should be a battle on moths above the city. No armor, and this time we'll allow weapons like crossbows and javelins. It will be spectacular, elves flying like birds, fighting in the sky. A little messy when one falls, but I have men who can clean it up."

The Regent shrugged. All eyes turned to Thyra.

"While I do agree a battle on flying moths would be spectacular," said Thyra, "I remind you that article eight of the Winnowing contract states that the Night Elves get to choose the time, place, and rules of the second contest."

Gorm's lips compressed to a thin line. "And what will those be, then?"

Thyra nodded slightly at Ali. "Astrid, will you explain the rules of the contest?"

"Of course." Ali crossed her legs, leaning back on the sofa with her arms spread out like she owned the place. "In the Shadow Caverns, we have no sun. No light to grow grass. There are no horses, no cattle, no beasts of burden of any sort. We have only the occasional goat and mushrooms. That's it. All Dokkalfar, young and old, must run or walk if they wish to travel. So, in honor of my people's humble lives, we will be hosting a foot race—"

"A foot race!" Gorm interrupted, laughing. "There must be fighting. How are elves going to die in a foot race?"

"Your Majesty," said Ali, cold as ice, "please allow me to finish."

Gorm nodded, fuming.

"We'll have a foot race. It will start on Bunker Hill and end in front of the Old State House. Elves may bring any weapons they like, as long as they do not shoot projectiles. Same rules as the melee." For the first time since we entered the barge, Ali's eyes met mine. "And this time, no magic. None whatsoever."

CHAPTER 18

ALI

Gorm's eyes narrowed with rage as I finished describing the rules of the foot race, and his impotent anger gave me a bit of satisfaction.

"Of course the Night Elves want to run." His voice cracked with anger. "That's what you do, right? Run and hide. You need to come up with a proper contest, not some nimby-pimby street scuttle."

I shrugged. "We're in charge of this contest, so you're just going to have to trust me when I say that plenty of elves are going to die. Believe me when I say you're not going to want to be in last place, although, given your age and physical condition, that is entirely possible."

Gorm's face turned nearly crimson. "Do not speak to a king with such insolence."

"Sir, let me remind you that earlier tonight you called a Shadow Lord a *hag* and a *bitch*. I will describe you however I damn well please."

Perhaps it was my imagination, but I thought I saw a flicker of a smile ghost across Galin's lips.

"Gods dammit!" shouted Gorm, throwing his mug across

the interior of the barge. It shattered above a velvet sofa, splattering the gold cushions with hot chocolate. After a moment of tense silence, he stalked over to the bar.

Next to me, Thyra whispered, "Nice work."

"Will two days be enough time to prepare?" I whispered back.

"Definitely."

I turned, looking out the windows and marveling at the view. Whorls of snow flittered through the air outside. Far below us, I could just barely see the lights of Boston. A quiet movement caught my eye, and I looked up just in time to see Galin slip out the door to the balcony.

He would be alone out there. This was a chance I had to take.

Quietly, I rose and slipped outside.

Galin was standing by himself at the far end of the balcony. He leaned against the gilded railing looking into the darkness.

Should I push him, then claim it was an accident? He was their greatest weapon. I'd seen it for myself, the godlike damage he could wreak on his enemies. He was like an angel of death.

Undoubtedly, it would be the best thing for my people if he were dead. Taking the High Elves' best fighter out would give us an enormous advantage in the Winnowing. Considering he'd gotten me thrown in prison, I owed him nothing.

But when he whirled to look at me, his golden eyes burning, I felt it again. That feeling of glass shattering in my heart. "Hello, Ali. Have you come to try to kill me again?"

"I've considered it."

"You won't be able to." His deep voice slid around me like a warm caress, and I breathed in the scent of wood smoke and sage.

"It would be best for the Night Elves if you were dead," I whispered.

Galin gave me a slow, seductive smile. The next thing I knew, he was standing before me, hands on either side of me, gripping the railing. He was boxing me in, giving me a look that was sensual, carnal. It was a gaze that slid into my soul, as though he could see every inch of my secret desire for him. In the freezing air, heat rippled off his body.

"The gods are dead," he said, "and nothing means anything, except this: we are bound to one another. I don't know why. Only the Norns truly know the ways of Wyrd. The link between our souls commands them to be together. If you try to sever the link, Wyrd fights back. You are mine and I am yours." His low voice heated my blood.

I clenched my jaw, trying to block out the intensity of his stare. This situation was all wrong, and I felt like my legs were about to give way. "Am I actually your mate?"

His eyes gleamed. "Can't you feel it?"

A vernal scent curled around us, and my body was growing warmer. I could feel it—like our souls were twined together. I ached to be near him. And that was what made me feel like my heart was breaking. I swallowed hard. "Maybe."

"So why are you so eager to see me dead? I thought we were allies."

"Oh, did you?" I spat. "So why did you fuck me over? You betrayed me. You told the Shadow Lords about us, that I helped their worst enemy. You knew *exactly* how that would turn out. With me in prison."

He shook his head slowly. "What are you talking about?"

"I was imprisoned in Audr Mine because of you. Forced into hard labor. You wrote a letter to the Shadow Lords, and that was the result. Since I received a marked lot, I've spent every moment with the Shadow Lords. I shouldn't even be talking to you now."

And yet, I was here like an idiot, because I was drawn to him. Because I could feel his soul calling to mine. I had to kill him, but I just wanted to be in his arms. When I was with him, it was like I could feel the world coming alive again.

Galin narrowed his eyes. "I wrote no letter, Ali."

I stared at him, frustration simmering. "Who the fuck wrote it, then?"

"You were imprisoned? Then how did you come find me in the Citadel?"

"What? *You* sent me into the mines to die. You said you'd come for me, and you didn't."

A muscle twitched in his jaw. "I've been trying to get to you. This helm stops me. I've been working to remove it, but it's enchanted with powerful binding magic. If I try to leave the Citadel or hurt my family, it shocks me. Gorm is terrified of what I'd do without it. As he should be."

A fluting voice cut him off: "Oh, Galin! What are you doing with that Night Elf?"

My stomach fell as I watched Revna saunter over to us.

"I'm sorry, did I interrupt something?" she said in her sing-song voice, her eyes narrowing suspiciously. "A lovers' tête-à-tête?"

Galin turned away from me, casually leaning back against the railing. "I do believe she was considering throwing me over the side."

Revna glared at him. "You're needed in the cabin," she said walking back towards the cabin.

Without another word, Galin stalked off, one hand by the hilt of his sword.

My thoughts were a storm of conflicting emotions, and I was left alone, looking out into the winter night. Above me, hundreds of giant moths flapped, black silhouettes against the already dark sky. The barge swayed slightly, like a boat on a gently undulating sea.

I felt like my soul was splitting in two. One half of me wanted to achieve my destiny, to fulfill the promise to my parents. The other half of me simply wanted to run away with Galin.

My heart was shattering, and I had to get ahold of myself. Gods, it would have been easier without this bond, without the Norns entwining our souls. It was easier when I had simply wanted him dead. Now, I had no idea what to make of myself. The North Star was supposed to kill Galin, to avenge our people. Without that, what was I?

I didn't want to let Wyrd dictate my life the way he let it. I wasn't like Galin—a relic from another time, a royal. He came from a time of living gods, of mysticism and awe. I'd grown up scrounging for scraps, living in caves and eating mushrooms.

We made our own fates in the caverns, and I intended for it to stay that way. Fuck the soul bond.

When you were born to be a king, of *course* you believed in fate. You believed you inherited a throne and a crown because the gods had decreed it must be so, not because you came from a long line of tyrants who took what they wanted. But what had Wyrd ever done for people like me?

I gripped the freezing railing, my palms sticking to it.

I didn't know what I would do now. All I knew was that *I* would write the story of my own life—not the Norns, and not Wyrd.

CHAPTER 19

GALIN

I slammed the door to my quarters and summoned a bit of magic to lock it behind me. I stalked toward my desk, muttering, "*Finnask,*" to uncloak my hidden spell books.

My body burned with fury. I was being played, and I had a good guess as to who might be playing me.

Whatever had happened reeked of Revna's influence. Had she come to my room disguised as Ali? I shuddered to think of what I might have done with her. In fact, that horrible thought had me nearly wanting to activate the helm to burn the idea away.

Whoever it was must have convinced a witch—a seidkonur —to change her appearance to look like Ali's doppelgänger. No, it could have been even easier. She wouldn't have had to get a seidkonur to help her, because my father could have done it.

Two strokes of Levateinn, Loki's wand, and he could make Revna look like anything. All he would need was a tiny bit of Ali to build off. And they had that, didn't they? Revna had cut off Ali's finger. A little leftover blood on the stones would do it.

Rage simmered. As soon as I defeated this helm, the royals would be dead, and I would rule as king. I traced my fingertips over the rune glowing on my chest.

I crossed to the window, staring absently at Boston's ruined skyline.

There had to be a way to break the spell that bound the helm to my skull. Every spell had its weakness, its fatal flaw.

Take my wall, for example, the very thing that had first led Ali to despise me. I'd spent months ensuring no elf could cross it, but I hadn't counted on vergr crystals. Totally inert, the wall was completely permeable to them. All a Night Elf had to do to cross into Midgard was toss one through to the other side and teleport. When I'd first constructed the wall, I hadn't known vergr crystals existed. The Night Elves had discovered them somewhere in the bowels of the earth only *after* they'd been imprisoned.

This was the problem with binding magic. There was always some edge-case, the magical equivalent of a security flaw. Like computer hackers long ago, a good sorcerer could find a way to break any spell. The trick was to think outside the box. What angle hadn't the makers of the Helm of Awe considered?

Magic wouldn't remove it. It couldn't be destroyed by physical means, only weakened a bit. This made sense. Any sorcerer worth their salt would have anticipated both of these approaches.

I turned from the window and began to pace the length of my room. There had to be something I wasn't thinking of, something that the creator of the helm hadn't considered. A secret weakness, an Achilles heel.

What if...

I stopped short in the center of my room. There was one

thing the helm couldn't prevent me from doing. It couldn't stop me from separating my soul from my body and ascending to the astral plane.

Quickly, I sat on the flagstone floor and, closing my eyes, allowed my soul to drift free. I hovered just above my corporeal form, looking down at myself. But the helm didn't hum; no bolt of white-hot magic threatened to fry my frontal lobes. This was to be expected. I wasn't trying to leave the Citadel or attack a member of my family.

I allowed my soul to drift out the window, then peered in at my body still cross-legged on the stones. The helm remained quiet, completely inert. It couldn't sense where my soul was located.

The next step was to test the family angle. Darkness descended as I allowed myself to ascend into the astral realm. All around me, the souls of elves flickered like stars.

I whirled, searching. After a few moments, I found the one I was looking for, hovering a few floors above me. I glided up.

Revna's soul floated in the center of her room. I imagined her future assassination. A quick knife to the heart, so that I might secure the realm. Normally, at that gruesome thought alone, the helm would have sprung to life and zapped me.

I flicked back to check the status of my body. It remained on the floor, the helm completely quiet.

I slipped back inside my body. Even as I opened my eyes, I was thinking about what this meant. The helm was clearly attached only to my corporeal body—my physical form. My soul could do whatever it wanted.

I smiled slowly. Perhaps I could collect my rat, Gormie, from the dungeons, pop his soul into my body, then take over his furry form. I'd have free range of Midgard. I didn't particularly want to be in the body of a rat, though. It didn't seem fitting for a prince, and I didn't think Ali would like it much either.

What other options did I have? I could become a lich again. Killing myself would almost certainly break the connection between the helm and my body. But as a lich, I'd forgotten the gods entirely, forgotten my life. I didn't want to forget again.

There was, it occurred to me, one other option. As I thought of it, I squeezed my eyes shut, rubbing my face in my hands. It was nearly as bad as becoming a lich. Possibly worse.

But as I mulled over the possibilities, it was the only one that seemed likely to work.

CHAPTER 20

GALIN

Carefully, I arranged the black candles in a small circle in the center of the room. Back in my lair in Cambridge, I'd had a whole box of them, but here in the Citadel, there were none. Instead, I'd jerry-rigged some table candles I'd stolen from the dining room and coated them with soot from the fireplace. Hopefully, that would work.

After the candles were placed into their positions, I sat in the center of the circle and propped a grimoire in front of me. With one hand, I flipped to the page of the summoning spell. With the other, I picked up a small iron dagger.

I drew a deep breath to center myself. I needed to cut my skin. This was the crucial step, but I didn't know if I could do it. I could easily withstand the pain, but the Helm of Awe might stop me from hurting myself as a member of the royal family.

There was only one way to find out.

Quickly, I drew the blade of the dagger across my palm.

I gritted my teeth, waiting for a magical blast from the crown, but none came. Apparently hurting oneself was allowed.

Blood dripped between my fingers. Carefully, I began adding a few drops to the wick of each candle. Summoning magic still required a *blot*—an offering to the gods. Even when they were dead.

Once each candle had been fed with my blood, I said, "*Kaun,*" and lit them. As they guttered with bloody wax, I turned to the grimoire and began to incant the spell.

The flames slowly stilled, and the runes on my chest burned with light. When I spoke the last word of the spell, the candles blazed up around me, blinding me.

I blinked until my eyes adjusted.

Now, the candles surrounded me tightly, glowing like the eyes of wild animals. Beyond the ring, I could see nothing. My bed, my desk, my window had all been replaced by a stygian darkness. A black mist swirled around me like the ink of a giant squid.

The spell had worked. I remained seated as the candles continued to burn. At this point, I just had to wait.

Suddenly, the candles blazed brighter, now taking on a purplish hue. The temperature dropped, and my breath misted.

Slowly, a form appeared in the mist. A dark shape that hovered at the edges of my vision. Frost spread across the iron blade in my hand like icy spider webs. Slowly, the creature inched closer, pale eyes glowing in the darkness.

"Galin." The shade spat my name like an insult. "Why have you summoned me?"

"I am here to make amends."

"Amends? From you? You *promised* that you'd raise our queen from the dead. Yet she still rots on her throne." The shade's eyes flashed, and it hissed, "I see your soul enjoys the warmth of a living body, you dishonorable bastard."

"That's not entirely true."

"It's not? You dare suggest that I cannot see your golden

hair or hear your beating heart? When we spoke last, you were dead—a lich—but now you are alive. You found the wand and used it to save yourself, but you did not honor your oath."

"I am here to do that now."

"And that is why you've confined yourself within a circle of power? I can smell the iron in the flames of your candles." The shade inched closer, its voice icy. "Blow out the tapers so we can become properly reacquainted."

"Not yet."

"Then I have nothing to say to you." The shade's body began to fade, slipping back into the swirling mist.

"Ganglati, wait."

The shade paused, his pale eyes fixing on me once again. "What did you call me?"

"Ganglati."

"I haven't heard that name in a thousand years."

"But that *is* who you are, isn't it? Ganglati, the lazy walker, chief manservant of Hela, Queen of the Dead?"

"My queen is dead. I serve no one."

"I am here to make you an offer."

"No. *You* fulfill your oath first."

Negotiating with the shade was proving more difficult than I'd imagined. "That is my desire, but in order to fulfill my oath, I need your help." I pointed at the Helm of Awe. "Levateinn was stolen from me. The one who took it bound this infernal crown to my head. If I move against him, its magic scalds my brain."

The shade didn't seem convinced. "I thought you were a powerful sorcerer."

"This magic, I cannot break—at least not with the tools currently at my disposal. The helm imprisoned me, but if I were free of it, then it would be a simple thing for me to steal back the wand. If you take over my body, then for a short time at least, the helm could be broken. Temporarily deactivated, with you in control. Then we can do what we must. And once I have Levateinn, I can return to your lands and revive your goddess."

Ganglati hovered just in front of the encircling candles. His eyes glowed bright in his shadowy form. "You *will* honor your oath, then?"

"Will you help me?"

The shade studied me, eyes shining in the darkness. "What do you propose?"

"Join forces with me. Help me steal the wand."

Ganglati laughed icily. "Impossible. I am dead. You've seen the iron wall that confines me to Hel." His eyes flashed. "Stop wasting my time. What you suggest is impossible."

"It's not impossible. Didn't you just say that I am a powerful sorcerer?"

I licked the tip of my thumb and index finger, then extinguished the candle nearest to me. Frigid black mist began to rush into the circle of candles.

The shade's eyes glowed brighter, like stars in the darkness.

I held his gaze as I spoke. "You see, the helm is bound to my body. Not to my soul. Step inside the circle and join me within *this* living body." I touched my chest. "Together, we can defeat the helm and retrieve Levateinn. Then, I will raise your queen."

CHAPTER 21

ALI

In the Citadel courtyard, a High Elf servant beckoned Thyra and me with a long finger. "Follow me. I will show you the way to your rooms."

As we followed him into the Citadel, Thyra spoke quietly. "Ali, can I put you in charge of collecting the—" She leaned close, whispering.

"Yes, of course. Is it okay if I have Bo assist me? The stunning spell has worn off."

"Whatever you need."

"I'll start tomorrow."

The halls of the Citadel were dark, but the guard held a lantern, and it cast warm light over rough marble walls.

"Thyra," I whispered. "You know about magic, right?"

"Some …" She replied noncommittally.

"What do you know about the Norns?" I asked.

She raised an eyebrow. "The Norns? Not very much. They cast our souls and weave our fates with the threads of Wyrd. They are said to live among the roots of Yggdrasill. But as far as I know, no elf has ever seen one."

We continued through the dark halls, the rough stone

dimly lit with flickering torches. It looked like a medieval castle in here, built of rough stone and low arches.

"Do you think the Norns died in Ragnarok?" I asked after a few moments of silence.

Thyra shrugged. "Maybe. I couldn't say. But without them, fate would no longer exist. So probably not."

I took a deep breath. Everything hinged on what I had to say next. "Hypothetically, if they were still alive, do you think someone could change the fate the Norns wove for them?"

Thyra gave me a long look. "Why the sudden interest in the Norns?"

"I was just curious."

"I doubt it. Like I said, no one has ever seen one—"

"Miss," the servant interrupted. "This is your room." He was looking directly at me, gesturing for me to enter.

As the servant unlocked the door, I turned again to Thyra. "Will you be alright on your own? I can accompany you to your quarters."

"I'll be fine," said Thyra. "Gorm wouldn't dare hurt me. I'll be perfectly safe."

Good to know. "Well, don't hesitate to stop by if you need anything."

As Thyra and the guard disappeared down the hallway, I pushed open the door to my room.

It was larger than I expected. It wasn't just a room, but an entire suite. I stood in a central living room with an oak table and sofas, but I could see a bedroom on one side and a private bathroom on the other. The walls were made of white stone, and an ornate carpet was spread out over the floor. Multi-paned windows overlooked the frozen city.

I poked my head into the bathroom. There was a sink, a tall mirror, and a clawfoot tub in the center. Finally, I crossed to the bedroom. I found a bed draped with red velvet curtains, and the same sleek stone walls. A tapestry depicting the goddess Freyja with long golden hair hung above a small hearth.

I also found that someone had delivered my things. Not that I'd brought very much, just a few changes of clothes and my gear, including my crossbow and collection of magical bolts. Everything was neatly arranged on a mahogany dresser.

I didn't think I'd held my crossbow since I'd first tried to steal Galin's ring. Picking it up, I checked the tautness of the string. Then, I inspected the bolts. Everything seemed to be as I remembered: anti-hex bolts, smoke bolts, and of course, a small quiver of eitr bolts.

I held up one of the eitr bolts, careful not to touch the tip. Eitr bolts were exceptionally lethal. In fact, one eitr bolt contained enough venom to kill five hundred elves. Even a grazing of the skin was enough to induce a permanent coma.

Putting the bolts down, I kicked off my shoes.

Thyra hadn't known anything about the Norns. And I'd been to the bottom of the Well of Wyrd myself. There hadn't been any old hags weaving fates or casting souls among Yggdrasill's roots. Just a pile of bones and a massive bloodthirsty squirrel. Was any of it real—my destiny?

I peeled off the rest of my clothes, then dropped onto my bed, hoping for sleep. But whenever I closed my eyes, Galin's face rose in my mind—his sensual mouth, his masculine jaw, his eyes the palest gold. His sly smile as he looked at me—the arrogance of someone who believed he'd one day be king.

I needed to get him out of my head.

Rising, I stalked to the bathroom, then stripped out of my bra and underwear and started filling the bath. When the tub was full and steaming, I slipped in, groaning softly as the hot water enveloped me.

I closed my eyes, allowing the heat to loosen my muscles. This was exactly what I'd needed. In the Shadow Caverns, we didn't have luxuries like tubs or showers. If we wanted to bathe, we had to boil water in buckets.

Picking up a purple bar of soap from the foot of the tub, I began to scrub at the dirt on my arms, tracing from my shoulders to my wrists. Lavender, I decided, was my new favorite scent.

I spread lather onto my shoulders, cleaning my neck and behind my ears. Soapy rivulets trickled between my breasts. I slipped back into the water, up to my neck, and rubbed at my chest to get the grime off.

I never want to leave this tub.

Once again, Galin's stupidly beautiful face rose in the hollows of my mind, and my pulse started to race. I would absolutely not think about how his body looked, about his golden skin stretched over taut muscles. And I would not imagine that subtle curve of his lips, or his cheekbones carved by the gods.

It wasn't my fault. How many years had it been since I'd been with a man? Two, three? The last time had been a drunk fling with a Night Elf named Sven. He was cute, but it had lasted a few minutes max.

I floated in the deliciously warm tub, the water lapping at my breasts. As I closed my eyes, I started to drift into a dream—one where Galin was in the tub with me, our bodies intertwined, sliding against each other. A low, appreciative growl escaped his throat, the sound trembling over my naked skin. My breath sped up, and I pressed against his body, reveling in the feel of pure steel under the soft skin. Warmth swooped into my belly, and I melted against him.

It was only Galin and me, our mouths open, tongues brushing, his hands caressing my ass, strong arms wrapped around me…

My eyes snapped open, and I found that my hand was starting to slide between my thighs.

I leapt up. *Nope. Nope. Not happening.*

Fucking Wyrd.

I jumped out of the tub, dripping wet. Nearly slipping on the bathroom tiles, I spun, Skalei suddenly tight in my fist ... but I had no idea what I was trying to attack. My own traitorous thoughts? Obviously, the tub was empty, because I was alone.

Naked and shivering, I thrashed around the bathroom, unclear on who I was angry at. Galin? The Norns? Myself for no longer having a purpose in my life?

And where the fuck was a bath towel?

At last, I found one folded neatly beneath the sink and wrapped it around me.

Then, I flung open the door just in time to see a portal expand. Magic crackled, and before I could move, the real Galin stepped casually into my room.

CHAPTER 22

GALIN

Water dripped from her silver hair, along her shoulders, down the curves of her breasts peeking above the towel. She looked like a nymph fresh from a deep forest pool. For an instant, I imagined what her legs might look like wrapped around my hips, like they had been on the battlefield.

I smelled lavender—and something more. A feral scent I couldn't place. My body stiffened.

With effort, I pulled my eyes away from Ali so I could concentrate. I looked to the window. "Sorry for the intrusion, but we need to talk.'

"You could have knocked," she shot back, "and come in the door like a normal person."

"That would have been a bad idea, obviously. I'll leave after we talk."

"Fine. Give me a minute." She stalked past me, toward the bedroom.

While she dressed, I crossed to a small mahogany table of tumblers and liquor and poured myself a whiskey. I let the smoky flavor roll over my tongue, wishing I could be alone in this room with Ali under very different circumstances.

When she returned, she was dressed in her usual black leather. She looked exhausted. "What do you need?"

"Your help stealing back Loki's wand."

"Again? We already did that."

"Levateinn is exceptionally powerful. We could use it to defeat an army. I could simply turn the High Elf troops into a school of fish. They'd slowly suffocate, no fighting necessary. Alternatively, I could temporarily transform the Night Elves into lions, and you could eat your foes alive."

She crossed her arms. "That is ... disturbing and enticing at the same time." She still seemed wary of me, but at least she was letting me speak.

Before I could reply, a loud knocking at the door interrupted us.

"Ali?" A woman's voice pierced the wood. "Can we talk?"

"Shit. I think it's Thyra. You need to leave."

Already, a key jingled in the lock. I didn't have time to scribe a portal. Instead, I slipped into the bedroom, mere seconds before the door opened. I left the door open a crack so I could listen.

"What do you want?" I heard Ali say. "I was just going to bed."

She's a feisty one, I'll give you that, whispered a deep voice in my head.

Shut up, Ganglati.

She has a fine figure, continued the shade. *Have you enjoyed her body yet?*

From the other room, Ali's voice rose. "*No*, you can't come in here."

I heard the faint tinge of fear in her voice, and my muscles tensed. I peered through the gap in the door, expecting to catch a glimpse of Thyra.

But it was an elf in a black cloak, a cowl shadowing her face. With a blade in her hand, she lunged toward Ali. My heart skipped a beat.

Ali dove out of the way of the dagger. As she did, she kicked upwards, knocking the dagger from the assassin's hand. It flew across the room and skittered under a chair. The assassin swiveled and kicked Ali back.

I tried to pull the door open to get to Ali, but the shade was taking over, controlling my body.

What are you doing? I screamed mentally.

The Night Elf might die. I haven't seen the transition from life to death in so long. How I've yearned for it.

The assassin held Ali by the throat, crushing her ability to call for Skalei, and I was immobilized, terror screaming in my mind. My legs were locked in place, muscles frozen.

Horror washed over me as I realized my mate was about to be murdered, and I couldn't do anything to stop it.

Let me go! I shouted at Ganglati.

All lives must end. The shade sounded casual.

I strained to move as the assassin lifted a blade to Ali's throat. Panic was ripping my mind open.

She was going to die.

I tried to look away, but Ganglati kept my eyes focused on Ali's throat. *I haven't seen a death in thousands of years*, he whispered excitedly.

He had taken over my body, but Ali was my light in the darkness, and I would get to her. I felt like ice had stiffened every part of me, and when I moved, it was like my muscles were being sliced with shards of glass. Still, I tried to rush for her before it was too late.

CHAPTER 23

ALI

The assassin lifted me by the throat, and the edges of my vision swam.

She leaned against me with her full body weight, pressing me into the wall. I could feel her free hand moving towards me. I didn't have to see the blade to know I was about to be stabbed.

With the last of my strength, I brought my knee up into the assassin's gut.

I couldn't see her face behind the hood, but I heard the grunt of pain. Her body spasmed, and I knew I'd knocked all the wind from her lungs. And then, most importantly, I heard the distinct clattering sound of a dagger hitting the floor.

She doubled over.

"Skalei."

She looked up as my blade appeared in my hand. That gave me the opening I needed. I lunged forward and plunged Skalei into her eye. Dead. Finally.

But before she could fall to the ground, Galin gripped her

by the head and twisted. The crack of her breaking neck echoed off the walls.

The assassin slumped forward, against me, then slid to the floor.

"Took your time to jump in," I said as I looked up at Galin. "I had actually already killed her, for the record."

"Ali, I couldn't move. The shade Ganglati paralyzed me."

I no longer had any idea what mystical gibberish he was banging on about.

"Well, I was fine on my own. As I said, I did kill her." Some of my pride seemed to be at stake here.

Galin crossed to the door and locked the deadbolt.

When he returned, he nodded at the body. "Who is it?"

The assassin lay face down on the floor, and I knelt to give her a better look. I rolled her over, then let the hood fall away, revealing her identity.

I'd expected to see golden hair, but this elf's hair was a dark brown. Wavy and thick, it draped over her face. I brushed it away. The elf's remaining eye stared up at me, lifeless. She was unquestionably dead, but that wasn't what interested me. It was the color—not gold, not silver, but a deep emerald green.

"It's a Vanir," I said at last.

Galin whistled low. "I didn't see any women when we were in Vanaheim, but you did kill their Emperor. The Vanir must have recognized you."

That again. "Right. I had hoped that might be water under the bridge."

"It could, in fact, explain why the Vanir came at all," Galin said thoughtfully. "And now both the High Elves and the Vanir want you dead. I can protect you from my family, but the entire kingdom of Vanaheim will be more complicated."

Galin began pacing the room, and I checked the dead elf's

pockets. I found them empty. Picking the dagger up from the floor, I tucked it back into her belt.

Then, I turned to Galin, but he was muttering something about full body protection charms.

"Galin," I said. "We have to get rid of the body. If she's found in my room, no spell will protect me. The penalty for killing an elf of another tribe is forfeiture of the Winnowing, if it happens outside the contest trials." I went to the nearest window and began to unlatch it. "We should throw her out the window."

"Ali." He gave me a lazy smile. "I'm not Marroc anymore. I'm not a lich. My magic is much more powerful now." He pulled off his shirt, revealing his chest and arms, thickly corded with muscle.

I stared at him. "What kind of magic are we talking about?"

Without answering, he traced a rune on his chest. It glowed with golden light, and then an electric sound crackled as a portal opened in the center of my room—a ring of sizzling energy with an inky black center. "There are more discreet ways to dispose of a body."

"Weird, but okay."

Galin flicked his fingers, and the portal rotated so that it hovered flat, about a foot above the floor. Then, he crouched down to pick up the body bridal style.

I stared as he dropped her in, and she plummeted into the darkness.

He flicked his fingers again, and the portal twisted back into a vertical position. "We should both leave before the Vanir send backup to find out what happened." Galin glanced at the window. "Sun's coming up already. Follow me."

He crossed through the portal just as I heard footfalls outside.

"Skalei." I still didn't know where the portal was going, but I leapt in anyway.

I landed in a forward roll, which turned out to be a terrible idea because Galin's portal had taken us outside. I rolled through a deep drift of snow.

I leapt up, frantically wiping snow from my face. "I'm fine," I said before he asked. I shook snow from my hair.

Galin was standing a few feet away, in front of an open grave. The Vanir corpse lay at his feet.

It seemed we were in a graveyard. Ancient stones jutted from the snow like a hag's teeth, and above us, the frozen branches of an elm speared the night sky. Bitter cold gnawed at my skin.

"Galin," I said. "I need you to tell me about the letter. The one that got me thrown into the mines for treason. You still haven't explained it to me. Did you expect me to die there?"

He looked confused. "I didn't send a letter. Of course I didn't want you in the mines. I was trying to get to you."

"So who wrote it?"

He shook his head. "I don't know yet. But Ali... you must realize at this point that I don't want you dead."

I bit my lip. My hatred for him had brought a strange sort of familiar comfort in the mines. I was almost reluctant to let go of it. No, it wasn't just comfort—it had given my life a purpose.

Without it? I had no idea what I'd do with myself.

But I had to admit—if he'd wanted me dead, he'd have killed me in the battle. And I supposed letters could be forged. "I guess it could have been written by someone else," I admitted.

"Ali, I can't stop thinking about you ... and with the gods dead, you are the only thing that has meaning for me anymore. We are bound, our souls entwined. I have no choice but to love you."

My breath left my lungs. "No choice?" Apart from the speed at which I was trying to adjust my conception of him, there was something about that particular point that bothered me. "No choice. You make it sound like a prison sentence. If you have no choice, it's not real, is it? If you take the magic away, maybe we have nothing in common. I can't talk about which rune will best stun a draugr, just as you wouldn't know how to slice an elf's throat without soaking your clothes in blood. What if it's not real?"

His expression had gone glacial. "It's not *fake.* That is a very limited understanding of the importance of fate, Ali."

I clenched my jaw. "I want the bond to be broken. It's the only way to know what's real."

His divine gold eyes now held a mournful expression. "I've seen what happens when Wyrd is ignored."

"You have?" Here he was, making things up again.

"My mother's soul was also bonded to another."

"Your mother?"

"Yes, I had one of those once. She died a long time ago."

This was the last thing I'd expected to come out of his mouth, and my heart twisted. When my parents had died, I'd been a wreck for months. "I'm sorry."

"Shhh, listen—" He pressed a finger to my lips. The wind gusted, and Galin moved so that he shielded me from the blowing snow. "Wyrd bound my mother to a human. Someone named Brian. She tried everything to escape her fate, even going so far as to marry another. But the Norns had spoken."

"And that's how she married King Gorm?" I breathed.

"Exactly. She tried to break free of Wyrd, but she couldn't. In the end, it destroyed her. Her life was empty, rotten, wrong without Brian. I vowed never to make the same mistake as her. Wyrd is unfair, cruel, but you cannot fight against it. In the end, fate always wins."

"What happened to your mother?"

"Gorm had her killed."

"Why?"

But I already guessed the answer. Galin's broad shoulders, his enormous hands. The complete lack of that stupid High Elf sing-song voice. It all made so much more sense now.

My jaw dropped open. "Your father *was* Brian. You're part human. That's why Gorm hates you. Right?"

Galin nodded. "And it's also why Sune and Revna despise me. I'm the physical manifestation of my mother's unfaithfulness, and I'm not even a pure elf."

"Why doesn't Gorm just disown you, then?"

The wind toyed with his golden hair. "That would require him to admit that she cheated, that he was a cuckold. To an elf like my father, that's far worse than having a bastard son."

"So, you're not really his heir?"

"No, but I will be king." Gently, he brushed the back of his knuckles over my cheeks. "So, do you understand now why we can't fight Wyrd?"

I drew in a deep breath, feeling like my heart had iced over. And that I needed it to ice over, or I'd drown. "I understand where you're coming from, but I just can't do it. I just can't accept that there's some magical bond that prevents me from choosing who I desire, who I love. That it was decided for me by a Norn. To me, that's not true love. It's a spell."

He pulled his hand away from my cheek, and a muscle worked in his jaw. He fell silent, the wind toying with his pale hair. "All right, then. If that's truly what you want, I will help you break the bond."

CHAPTER 24

GALIN

I sat at my desk, watching the first rays of the sun creep over the Boston skyline. I was exhausted, but my thoughts raced wildly. I knew I needed to think, to come up with some kind of plan, but I was simply too tired to focus.

Well, that was quite the night, Ganglati whispered from some deep recess in my mind. I tried not to think about what he might find while rummaging around in there.

I really don't have time for you, I replied.

You promised—you vowed your soul, you gave me an oblation.

And I will fulfill that promise.

Suddenly, the fingers in my hand clenched, my bicep contracted, and I found my fingernails piercing my own palm, drawing blood.

Ganglati, I snapped inwardly. *It's 5 a.m. Even if I wanted to, I couldn't help you right now. King Gorm is asleep in his quarters, surrounded by twenty guards, each armed with the most lethal hexes. If I teleported into his room, I'd be struck down in seconds. If I'm dead, I can't help you.*

Construct a spell to protect yourself, he replied.

Again, my fist tightened involuntarily. I was beginning to seriously regret inviting the shade to share my body.

I could do that, but remember, Gorm also has Levateinn. It would overpower any protection spell I could construct. We need to take a stealthy approach. Steal it from him without him noticing. We would do better with Ali's help.

The shade didn't answer, but my muscles didn't clench any tighter, which I took to mean that he understood.

I rose and pulled the curtains closed before I stalked over to my bed. I threw myself on it, not bothering to undress. Sleep was more important, and I probably had only an hour left of it.

As soon as I closed my eyes, Ali's visage came to me. Dripping wet, fresh from the bath, her silver hair draped over her towel.

I wanted to pull the towel off her.

Why had I told her I would help her break the bond between our souls? I felt as if someone had hollowed out my chest. But perhaps I'd do anything she asked if it made her happy.

I closed my eyes again, determined not to think of her. Sleep—that was the crucial thing. But just as I was drifting off, someone knocked loudly on my door.

My eyes snapped open, and I snarled. I instantly looked to the runes I'd drawn on the door frame. They glowed softly. The door was locked.

I slipped out of bed and snatched a dagger from my desk. The knock sounded again. Louder. Urgent.

"Who is it?"

"Sune and me," Revna replied.

I groaned. "I was sleeping."

"The king asked us to talk to you."

With a quick flick of my fingers, I unlocked the door.

Revna and Sune strode in like they owned the place.

Revna plopped herself onto the sofa, while Sune began to wander aimlessly around my room. Between the wandering and his vacant expression, he could almost have been mistaken for a draugr.

"How well do you know the Night Elf?" said Revna.

Every one of the muscles in my body tensed. "Which Night Elf?"

Revna held up her right hand, then bent down her ring finger. She grinned, raising her eyebrows. "The one whose finger I cut off. I thought I saw you canoodling on the barge."

"Don't be absurd."

She leaned forward suddenly, like a snake striking. "She might end up injured if you don't tell us what we want to hear. Father wants to know what the Night Elves are planning."

Her voice was like nails scraping inside my skull. "He can ask them himself."

"Sune, make him talk."

Suddenly, Sune was by my side. He tugged at the helm, and it began to grow hot, sizzling.

Anger started roiling in me, and I had a very vivid image of myself hurling them off a Citadel tower.

"You're going to have to do what I say," Revna trilled.

Do you need my assistance? asked Ganglati. *I can take over and temporarily deactivate the helm. A short break from the Helm, and we can hurt them.*

No. I don't want them to know that I've found a way to sometimes break the spell.

As you wish.

I arched an eyebrow. I wouldn't share any information with them even if I knew it. "I only know what you know. The Night Elves are planning some sort of footrace."

"There has to be more than that," she said. "They're not stupid."

I rose, towering over my siblings. I felt a flash of satisfaction as they both shrank away from me. "As soon as I know anything, you'll be the first to hear," I lied. "Now get the fuck out."

I would end them both soon enough, when they least expected it.

CHAPTER 25

ALI

I rubbed my eyes as sunlight streamed into my bedroom. I glanced at a clock on the bedside table and, finding it was nearly eight o'clock, leapt up—breakfast was in ten minutes. After washing my face and changing into my leather outfit, I hurried down to the mead hall.

I found the hall full of elves and, more importantly, the scent of food. Instead of servers, there was a buffet: a table piled with pastries, platters of hot eggs and sausages, even some fresh fruit.

I'd been missing out on so many things in the caverns...

I was piling sausages on my plate when Bo sidled up to me. "Have you tried this?" He held up a mug full of a steaming black liquid.

I sniffed it, not recognizing the smell. "What is it?"

"It's called *coffee*."

"Coffee?" Something about it triggered a distant memory. When I was a child, my mother had told me stories about it—a hot drink made of beans that humans had loved. As a concept, it sounded pretty strange, but according to her stories, the humans had worshiped it like a god.

I'd never actually drunk coffee myself, though, and neither had my mother. After Ragnarok, supplies had immediately run out, and it was impossible to obtain.

I sniffed the mug again. "Do you think this is actually coffee?" Whatever it was, it smelled amazing.

"No idea." Bo pointed at a tall silver contraption on a nearby table. "I just got it out of that."

I put my plate of sausages down and hurried over to the coffee dispenser, then filled a cup and took a small sip. The flavor was not at all what I'd expected. Bitter and acidic. A bit like the juice of a rancid portobello mushroom. Discreetly as I could, I spat the rest of the mouthful back into the mug.

"What do you think?" asked Bo, grinning a bit too broadly.

Cheeky bastard knows it tastes worse than bat piss. "It's not ... not what I expected. I thought it would taste good." I couldn't keep the disappointment from my voice.

"Right? The humans had super weird taste in food. Have you ever had haggis?"

"No."

"Well, how about I tell you about it over breakfast?"

I snatched up my plate of sausages and followed Bo to a nearby table. He sat down with his coffee cup warming his hands, waiting for me to get settled.

Then, he looked me dead in the eyes. "So, you threatened to kill me."

I was beginning to realize I overestimated everyone's ability to designate things as *water under the bridge*. You assassinate an emperor, you threaten to kill a friend, and it turns out people don't simply forget it. Which, frankly, was deeply inconvenient for me.

"Sorry about that; I didn't have much of a choice." I held his gaze. "I was worried you could misinterpret the fight."

"And why was that?" Bo leaned forward, maintaining eye

contact. I had to give him some credit. It took serious balls to interrogate a professional assassin like this. "Do you know that I happen to know your brother, Barthol?"

My jaw tightened. "What?"

Bo took a sip of his coffee, grinning conspiratorially. "I was sent to the mines a week ago. The week before that, I was working with your brother. I got caught. He did not."

"Wait, you're saying Barthol is—"

"Working as a smuggler? Yup."

It didn't make sense. Barthol did things by the book; he wasn't one to break laws unless ordered to by the Shadow Lords. If anyone accidentally overcharged him in our market, he let them know immediately. "But why?"

"After you got sent to the mines three weeks ago, Barthol was kicked out of Sindri. No one would hire him. Except for my boss. Barthol has some valuable skills."

I narrowed my eyes at Bo. "You're blackmailing me, aren't you? If I don't tell you about Galin, you're going to rat Barthol out? Get him sent to the mines, too?"

Bo's grin widened. "How little you think of me! But yes, your low assessment is entirely accurate."

Fucker. I didn't know if this was true or a lie, but it had unnerved me anyway. I took another sip of my coffee, forgetting that I'd spit into it. "Skalei."

In one graceful swing, I slammed the blade through the center of Bo's mug. The ceramic shattered, and hot coffee sprayed all over his shirt.

"Look, you conniving shit. I work for the Lords of the Shadow Caverns. I am a trained assassin. Fuck with Barthol and it's not coffee that'll be soaking your chest. There will be no more talk of Galin. No more talk of Barthol. Are we clear?"

Bo simply gawked, his mouth half open.

"I'll take that as a yes. Now, let me drink my disgusting

coffee in peace." I took a long sip, indicating that the conversation was over.

I was beginning to understand the humans' infatuation with this bitter drink. It was starting to make me feel alive.

* * *

Bo left, ostensibly to change his shirt, and I was able to eat my breakfast in peace. A few minutes later, a group of guards entered the hall and announced the arrival of King Gorm. He, Revna, and Sune sat at their usual table on the dais. I didn't see Galin at all.

When someone called my name, I looked up to see Thyra beckoning me. After grabbing a roll and refilling my coffee cup, I hurried to join her.

As I sat, she stared at the mug in my hand. "Are you drinking coffee?"

"Yup. It's actually amazing. I could eat nails."

Thyra shook her head. "Well, I guess it's better than espresso shots."

Before I could ask her what an espresso shot was, Gorm spoke. "Thank you all for coming to breakfast. I hope everyone slept well. The Night Elves will be holding the next contest. Lord Thyra will explain the details."

Next to me, Thyra stood. "Thank you, King Gorm." She turned to face the assembled elves. "I have already told your leaders the details of the contest, but fortunately, it is quite simple. A short footrace. We will run from Bunker Hill to the Old State House. I will reveal the exact route at the start of the race. As with the melee, hand to hand combat will be acceptable, but ranged weapons will not be allowed. Magic is strictly forbidden. The first two hundred twenty-five elves to finish will go on. The rest will be executed." A heavy silence fell over the hall. "We will race tonight at sundown."

"Tonight?" King Gorm interjected. "You told us in three days."

Thyra shrugged. "I changed my mind."

He spluttered before finally saying, "You can't do this."

Thyra smiled. "Oh, but I can."

And as she sat down again, I found myself hoping with a shiver of dread that neither Galin nor I would be among those executed tonight. I may have come up with the plan, but it was going to be a close thing to survive the race.

CHAPTER 26

GALIN

By the time I got down to the mead hall, it was nearly empty—just a few servants putting away dishes and pastries.

"Where is everyone?" I asked a servant as I snagged the last black currant scone.

"On the roof, Your Highness."

"On the roof?"

"They're exercising or something, my lord. Didn't you hear? There's going to be a contest tonight. A race."

"Tonight," I repeated, still not quite making sense of it. It seemed too soon.

With the scone still in my hand, I hurried up the Citadel's many flights of stairs until I reached the roof.

I found it awash with elves. A group of High Elves fought with practice swords, while Night Elves sparred bare-handed. Elves of all three tribes could be seen jogging around the path that ringed the parapets, warming up their legs.

"Galin!" I heard Revna shout.

I spotted her and Sune stepping down from the running

track. Revna was dressed like an athlete, in shorts, and a bejeweled dagger hilt protruded from a sheath at her waist.

She sidled up to me. "Have you learned anything about tonight's contest?"

I shook my head. "I was sleeping."

She rolled her eyes in annoyance. "Well, why don't you ask your little tunnel swine girlfriend?" She pointed to a group of Night Elves standing on one of the walkways. In the center, Ali was talking quietly with Thyra and Ilvis.

"How about I throw you into the Well of Wyrd?" The shock of heat to my skull was worth the fear in her eyes, even if it was just for a moment.

I turned to walk away from her, prowling over the parapets, but my gaze was on Ali. Her tight black leather showed off every curve, and she'd pulled her hair into a ponytail. I watched as she called Skalei to her. With a flick of her wrist, she tossed the blade high into the air. It spun and sparkled in the sunlight like a majorette's baton. When it fell back down, she effortlessly caught it.

She wasn't like any of the High Elves. She was strong, confident, lethal, and determined to make her own way. She would also kill me if it weren't for our bond. She seemed to feed off a yearning for vengeance.

She flipped the dagger again, even higher this time. If she miscounted the rotations, reached out at the wrong time, she could cut herself deeply, but she didn't. Her hand flashed out at just the right moment, effortlessly snatching the blade from the air.

I could have watched her all afternoon, but I knew this was also a chance to study the opposition.

I began to scan the contingent of Vanir, practicing on the dark stone cap that covered the Well of Wyrd. They'd split into two groups and were taking turns throwing a javelin back and forth. One group would throw the javelin, and as it arced through the air, the other would stand in its path, diving out of the way at the last moment like they were playing a strange game of chicken.

Why were they throwing javelins when ranged weapons weren't allowed? My spine stiffened as I wondered if they were going to come after Ali again. They still wanted revenge for their slaughtered Emperor.

A hawk—the one I'd seen perched on the Regent's shoulder—circled above the Vanir and watched as they tossed the javelin back and forth. Studying them, I noticed another subtlety to their game: each time they threw the javelin, the two groups moved a little closer together, increasing the difficulty.

Then, a particularly large Vanir picked up the javelin. Rearing back, he hurled it at the other side. It spun, shooting through the air like a missile, and the Vanir on the opposite side barely had time to dive out of the way. They leapt up, shouting obscenities. Apparently, this was a bridge too far, even for them.

The hawk swooped, screeching. Without warning, a Vanir warrior hurled the javelin at the opposing team, and he narrowly missed impaling another of his tribe.

More shouting and cursing. The hawk continued to screech.

They are insane.

I started towards the Vanir. By the time I approached, they'd set aside all pretext of sportsmanship and simply launched into a brawl. The two sides charged each other. A warrior snatched up the javelin and hurled it just as another Vanir tackled him.

The javelin flew out of his grip. Aimed much too high, it spiraled into the sky like a rocket. The two groups of Vanir clashed, and I heard the crack of a jaw shattering as the big

RUINED KING

Vanir punched a smaller warrior. Thinning the competition for us. What did they think they were doing?

Around the brawling Vanir, the Night Elves and High Elves watched, engrossed.

Movement flickered above me as the javelin descended again. And something else, I realized, squinting. The hawk racing after it. Diving, silent as a ghost.

In a blur, the hawk intercepted the javelin, knocking it, redirecting its path with a flash of talons.

Now, it flew directly towards Ali. My heart went still.

"Ali!" I shouted.

Too late. She spun, but there was no time to dodge, and the javelin plunged into her thigh.

She screamed, clutching her leg. Around her, Night Elves stood in shock.

I charged across the rooftop, my heart in my throat, blood roaring in my ears. "Keep her still! Don't let her move!" As I passed a guard, I yelled at him, "Get the royal doctor!"

I was almost to Ali's side when a trio of Night Elves cut me off. Thyra, Ilvis, and a large Night Elf I didn't recognize.

"Not one more step," said Thyra.

Anger roiled. I wanted to rip their heads off. "She's going to bleed out!"

Thyra held up a hand. "We'll deal with this on our own."

I wanted to fling her off the roof to get to Ali, but my interference could make things even worse. They already suspected her of consorting with the enemy.

The large Night Elf pointed a sword at my chest. I sized him up. He was large, but not as big as me. I wanted to shove him out of the way—into the Well of Wyrd, preferably.

Don't cause problems for your Night Elf, whispered Ganglati. *If you're distracted by her misfortunes, you'll never steal the wand.*

Fuck off, Ganglati.

A group of Night Elves surrounded Ali, blocking my view

of her. My heart ached. I desperately wanted to be by her side, to do something to help her.

I spoke to Thyra, using the calmest voice I could manage. "I've sent for a doctor. Will you at least allow her to get medical help?"

Thyra nodded. "I'll permit it."

I let out a long breath. The royal doctor was highly trained. I felt a sense of relief knowing that Ali would be in her care.

I turned away from the Night Elves, shadows sliding through my thoughts. I'd seen the hawk interfere with the javelin. That could be no coincidence. This had been a second assassination attempt. The Vanir were determined to kill Ali; they didn't give a fuck about the Winnowing.

I would find the ones who had given the order. The Regent could run now, but when I caught him, he'd regret the day he was born.

CHAPTER 27

ALI

When I first opened my eyes, I didn't know where I was. All I knew was that I was in a bed, but it wasn't a familiar one. The paint on the ceiling was a deep blue flecked with stars, and the air smelled strangely antiseptic.

I lifted my head high enough to see windows framed by white muslin curtains. I wasn't in my room, and the sunlight meant it wasn't the Shadow Caverns.

"Hello?" I called out.

No one answered.

I was very tired, but I tried to sit up anyway. Instantly, pain lanced up my leg, and I flopped flat on my back.

I remembered bits and pieces of the morning—drinking coffee for the first time. Then, a few minutes later, I'd had to threaten Bo. Again. After that, it went fuzzy. My mind felt mushy, like half my brain had been replaced with stale porridge.

I concentrated and managed to scrounge up a few more memories. They were hazy, but I was certain I'd been outside. There had been lots of elves. I was pretty sure Galin had been shouting...

I shut my eyes tight as I tried to bring the thoughts into focus, but all I could see was his golden hair, his piercing eyes. He'd been worried about me.

"Miss?" said a melodious voice.

I opened my eyes. An elf stood beside me. She wore a gray cotton smock, and her golden hair was pulled up tight against her head. A High Elf.

Am I a prisoner? Do I need to call Skalei?

I tried to sit up, but the same excruciating pain kept me from moving more than a few inches.

"Stay still," said the High Elf in dulcet tones.

Considering I couldn't sit up, I decided to opt for a less bloody approach. "Who are you? What happened to me?" *Gods, it even hurts to talk.*

"My name is Budli. I'm the royal doctor of the Citadel. I've been looking after you since the accident."

"What accident? Where am I?"

"You were injured on the roof of the Citadel."

The mention of an injury and the roof of the Citadel brought forth a rush of fresh memories. Now, I very clearly remembered standing in a group of Night Elves. Something had fallen from the afternoon sky and slammed into me like a bolt of lightning. Galin had been shouting. Thyra had been there...

"I need to speak to Thyra," I said.

"Not yet. You need to sleep."

I could feel panic growing in me. "What time is it?"

"Nearly six in the evening."

I gasped, the foot race was going to start in less than twenty minutes. "I have to get up. I can't stay here."

"Absolutely not. You must rest. Your tendons are shredded. That is my medical assessment."

"If I don't go to Bunker Hill, I'll be out of the Winnowing."

"That's nice, dear." The doctor leaned over me and placed a hand firmly on my shoulder. Despite her words, her voice had taken on a malevolent tone. "But you're staying here."

Behind her, the air began to flicker. I struggled to sit up even as the doctor leaned over me, both of her hands on my shoulders, holding me down. Pain screamed up my thigh.

"Tunnel elf," she whispered. "You're not going anywhere."

Light flashed behind the doctor, and the scent of ozone filled the room as a portal split the air. She spun with a shriek.

Galin stepped from the portal, his blond hair whirling around his head like a lion's mane. The doctor began to step back towards the door.

"Prince Galin," she sputtered.

"Get out." His voice had a lethal edge.

The doctor turned, fleeing. Galin followed after her, and I heard the sound of a struggle, then a door being slammed shut. A moment later, he stalked back into the room, slammed the door, and bolted it.

"What did you do to her?" I asked.

He shrugged. "Locked her in a utility closet." His eyes fixed on mine. "Sorry about that. I thought she was trustworthy. What did she do?"

"She was aggressive and weird, but I'm fine. What exactly happened today?"

"You don't remember?" he asked, blinking.

"Was I hit by a bolt of lightning?"

The corner of his mouth twitched. "Don't be absurd. What are the chances of that? No, it was a hawk interfering with the trajectory of a javelin to injure you. Much more normal." He dropped the sarcastic tone and sighed. "I really don't know what the fuck is happening, but I think it was another assassination attempt from the Vanir."

"A hawk ... what?"

"The Vanir tried to kill you, again. They threw a javelin. A hawk swooped in and knocked it off course. The javelin hit you in the thigh, and you nearly bled to death."

As he spoke, more memories jogged loose. Tossing Skalei. A wet *thunk*. Stumbling like I'd been kicked by a horse. But there had been so much blood and pain ... I remembered my people standing over me, telling me to stay with them. And, distinctly, from across the parapet, a Vanir warrior had *grinned* at me.

Galin strode to the edge of the bed. "Do you think you can stand?"

"Hel if I know," I mumbled, trying to sit up again, but pain shot through my leg, like it was being ripped open again. I stifled a moan, biting my lip. I'd trained to work when I was hurt, but I wasn't sure my leg was even functioning properly.

"Wait. I've got something that might help." Galin reached into his jacket pocket and produced a small orange container. Twisting off the cap, he dumped two pills into my palm.

"What is it?"

"Vicodin. It's like lidocaine but for the whole body."

"Oh, right ... stuff that makes you go numb." I quickly swallowed the pills. As I waited for the medicine to take effect, I asked, "What else did I miss?"

He scrubbed a hand over his jaw. "Not much, actually. Apart from your attempted murder, the day was uneventful. There was the avian assassination attempt, then people ate lunch, and now all the elves have traveled to Bunker Hill."

"I have to join them. If I stay in bed, I'm out of the Winnowing. If I don't participate, I'll be executed."

"I know." He nodded grimly. "That's why I'm here. Try testing your leg now."

This time, when I sat up, the pain wasn't as sharp. More

like a dull throbbing than a dagger jabbed into my femur. I gritted my teeth. "It hurts, but it's manageable."

I began to stand, but my leg wouldn't work properly. I flapped my arms as I started to lose balance, but Galin caught me before I fell, and I slumped against his steely chest. He looped a powerful arm around my waist, then held me firmly as I tried to walk. But my leg kept buckling.

"Galin." My voice cracked as I realized the implications of not participating. "I don't think I can do it. My leg is shredded."

I felt a tear sliding down my cheek. The Vanir had won. If I didn't participate, I was as good as dead. The bottom fifty percent of runners were to be executed.

Carefully, Galin helped me sit on the edge of the bed. Then, he knelt. "Let me see."

He pulled the hem of my hospital gown up, lifting it above my thighs. In the center of my leg, a jagged gash had been stitched shut with black thread.

"Let me have a look at the wound."

I nodded.

He grimaced. "Looks deep, but it doesn't seem to be infected, just inflamed, I think. If I wrap it up, that'll help." He looked up at me with pain in his eyes. "But even with the Vicodin, it's going to hurt a lot. Are you sure?"

"Go for it."

Galin stood quickly and hurried across the hospital room. After a minute of rummaging through a supply cabinet, he returned with bandages and a roll of medical tape. As he worked on my leg, warmth spread from where his hands touched my skin, and the pain subsided. He leaned in close as he worked, a strand of his hair brushing against my thigh. I stared at the masculine perfection of his powerful shoulders.

You know what? It was nice to have someone taking care of me.

"Okay," he said after a minute or two. "Now, can you try standing?"

When he helped me up this time, it didn't feel like someone was twisting a knife in my muscles. Even better, I was able to take a few tentative steps.

Smiling, I turned back to Galin. "Thank you. That's a lot better."

"Is everything okay in there?" came a male elf's voice, followed by quieter, sharp whispering. I wondered if someone had let the insane doctor out.

"I'm fine!" I shouted back, stalling for time.

"I really must check on the patient! The King has asked that I see to it personally."

I looked to Galin. "Can you get us out of here?"

In the next heartbeat, he was scribing the portal spell, and I was leaping through to the next trial.

CHAPTER 28

GALIN

I stepped out of the portal and into a snowy alley. Ruddy evening sunlight slanted over the snow, painting it with orange. The shouting of elves echoed nearby, but I couldn't see anyone. If any High Elves spotted me helping Ali, I would have a lot of explaining to do. Mentally, I reviewed what I knew of this particular trial. No magic allowed, no throwing projectiles. It was to be a race—nothing more, nothing less.

I was starting toward the sound of the elves when Ganglati whispered in my ear, *When are you going to talk to her?*

Soon, but not right now. I'm just trying to keep her alive.

The shade fell silent.

I crept toward the opening of the alley until I could see the white marble obelisk that loomed high above us atop Bunker Hill, gleaming gold in the setting sun. Before Ragnarok, it had been a historic monument in the center of the Charlestown neighborhood—a giant tower built to celebrate one of the first battles of the American Revolution. Back then, the colonists had held the hill through three assaults and killed nearly eleven hundred British soldiers while losing fewer than five hundred of their own men. I hoped that, like the colonists of 1775, the Night Elves had devised a plan that gave them an advantage.

If they had, I couldn't imagine what it was.

At the moment, I could see the three tribes of elves huddling around the foot of the obelisk, waiting for the challenge to start.

Ali sidled up next to me. "What's the plan?"

"You need to join the Night Elves before anyone sees you with me," I whispered. "In the meantime, I'll join the High Elves."

Ali started forward, limping slightly. Worry tightened my throat as I watched her head into the snow, injured and alone. Surely, she'd incorporated some lethal trickery into the mysterious footrace the Night Elves had organized.

"Wait," I called after her. "What are you planning? You do have a plan, right?"

"Of course we have a plan."

"Care to share?"

She narrowed her eyes, then simply put a finger to her lips. "If I told you, I would have to kill you." She started back into the snow, but after a few steps, she slowed, turning back to me. She spoke in a near whisper, like she was afraid someone might hear her. "I'll give you one hint, okay?"

I nodded.

"Bring a torch."

I arched a quizzical eyebrow, then nodded again. I had no idea what she was talking about, but I would bring a torch, even though the warning itself unnerved me.

As she limped away through the snow, the sun dipped below the horizon. A violet dusk began to settle over Bunker Hill. *What was the torch for?* I stood still, trying to puzzle it out. It wasn't night out yet; we wouldn't need it to see.

Unless—

"Oh no."

* * *

I REACHED the crowd of elves just as a spell shot into the air. With a crack, it exploded like a firework. A Night Elf in a striped official's shirt yelled at the top of his lungs, "Go, go, go!"

Around me, Vanir, Night Elves, and High Elves surged forward. We were already starting, apparently.

I broke into a sprint, my feet kicking up clouds of snow as we careened down the hill in an enormous wave. Around me, some of the others were sliding in the snow, tripping over each other. We were competing not only against the Night Elves, but against each other. Half of all the runners would be executed. I spotted some distinctly unsportsmanlike behavior—kicking the fallen, throwing elbows.

"Galin!" called out Revna's lilting voice. I turned to see her coming up behind me as we reached the bottom of the hill. "Where have you been?"

I shrugged. "Here and there."

The rest of the tribes had joined us now, and we ran together, the competition fierce and fast. A group of three Vanir passed close to us, and Revna emitted a little chirp of excitement.

She rushed forward, her dagger gleaming. She struck, and one of the Vanir fell, clutching his lower back. He shouted to his companions, and they slowed, reaching for their weapons, but Revna danced out of their way.

"Gods, this is fun!" shouted Revna gleefully as she rejoined me.

I pumped my arms, focusing only on the race. "Save your

energy, sister," I said in a harsh whisper, just loud enough that only she could hear.

There would be worse things to fight than the Vanir today.

* * *

A MINUTE LATER, we raced down Winthrop Street and past the Old Training Field. In the 18th century, it had been a practice area for colonial militias. Now, it lay frozen under the snows of Ragnarok.

We were just turning onto Park Street when I heard the first guttural shouts. Even though I'd been expecting them, my skin crawled.

"Galin," said Revna, still running next to me, "what's that sound?"

The reason why Ali had suggested torches. And in the next moment, Revna understood the reason for herself.

"Draugr!" she shouted.

A ripple of fear was already passing through the running elves. Even if they'd never actually seen one in the flesh, the bestial shouts of the draugr were enough to turn anyone's blood to ice. Cries of "Draugr!" began to fill the air.

I glanced over my shoulder. Undead corpses poured from the alleys behind us. I turned, watching with a feeling of nausea as a draugr descended on an injured Vanir. Their shouts became a frenzy of feral screams. Blood sprayed the frozen street.

The draugr paused for a moment, but the taste of blood sent them surging forward the next, teeth gnashing, ravenous cries echoing in the frigid air.

But it wasn't the sound of draugr that chilled me to the core. It was a woman's scream—a voice I immediately recognized.

I spun in time to see Ali fighting a group of Vanir. Even as the draugr bore down, the dark-haired warriors had surrounded her. With my heart slamming, I raced across the street to help her.

I saw Skalei flash as Ali stabbed a Vanir in the neck, but there were too many for her to take alone, in her state. Ten at least. One of them pushed her from behind, and she stumbled. A dagger glinted in the evening light as one of the warriors lunged.

But I'd reached her just in time. I drove my shoulder into the Vanir's chest, sending him crashing into a snowbank. Another leapt on me, but I threw him off. Even as we fought, the draugr gained on us.

I heard Ali call Skalei. She fought them in a frenzy of whirling snow and silver hair, ducking and slashing, dagger glinting. As one after another attempted to flank her, I snapped their necks.

When her attackers all lay dead, I held my hand out to her. "Are you hurt?"

"I don't think so," she said, panting. She started forward, then stumbled, clutching her injured thigh. Then, with wide eyes, she turned to look at the draugr. They were only fifty feet away, barreling forwards in a cannibalistic frenzy of leathery skin.

Adrenaline coursing through me, I grabbed one of the dead Vanir by the legs and spun round like a shot-putter, throwing him at the incoming horde. They slowed to eat him, buying us time.

Ali was gripping her thigh, and she'd sliced her pant leg open to look at her injury. She gritted her teeth, grunting. The stitches had ripped open, and blood pumped from the wound. She wouldn't be able to run anymore.

Panic coiled through my mind.

"Galin," she snarled. "I can't run. You need to go."

As if I'd leave her.

My heart hammered as I glanced back at the draugr, who had almost finished consuming the Vanir I'd thrown their way. Twenty seconds at best before they were upon us.

I crouched down, then scooped Ali up. She grunted as I moved her, but she gripped me tightly.

I broke into a sprint, flying down State Street. I didn't have time to consider what would happen when the High Elves realized I was helping her, but I was going to carry Ali to the Old State House if it was the last thing I did.

Five minutes later I was racing down the icy remains of Interstate 93 with Ali tight in my arms, the horde of draugr hot on my heels. Ali clung to me, her arms wrapped around my neck.

We crossed the Zakim Bridge, my feet slamming against the frozen pavement, and I careened down toward the Central Artery. This was a massive tunnel the humans had constructed before Ragnarok, and it now lay empty, icy ruins of another time.

I sprinted inside, starting to catch up to the other elves. Darkness enveloped me until the shadows were completely impenetrable.

"Ali. I'm going to need your help. I can't see a thing."

Her silver eyes shone in the darkness. "Just keep going straight. I'll tell you if anything gets in your way. I see people moving up ahead. I think we're catching up to the slowest elves."

Icy air filled my lungs, and I clutched Ali close. But the draugr were moving fast, too. Behind us, their voices began to echo off the walls as they entered the tunnel.

Worst of all, I thought I heard them in front of us, too.

"This isn't good," I said between breaths.

"There are more up ahead."

Suddenly, the tunnel echoed with the screams and shouts

of elves in front of us. I was starting to understand the plan. The Night Elves could see down here just fine, but everyone else was practically blind.

In front of me, I spotted the exit ramp leading out to Government Center, the shortest route to the Old State House. At its base, a second pack of draugr had descended on the approaching elves.

I slowed as I tried to devise a plan. "This is really the plan you came up with, Ali?"

She shot me a sharp look. "I know it's not pretty, but the point was to win, so that the Night Elves can live."

Fair enough.

I stopped looking around the tunnel. I needed a bigger weapon, or something I could light on fire. Fear condensed in my veins, as I heard the draugr closing in. "What are you doing?" she asked.

"Trying to save us. I didn't have time to grab a torch. You don't have anything flammable, do you?"

"No. The plan was for Night Elves to avoid them with our night vision."

"Well, I can't exactly use a fire spell with the no magic rule." I spun, trying to scan the shadowy tunnel interior. It wasn't much to look at. Rusty husks of ancient cars, chunks of concrete, ancient signage. Nothing I could use to start a fire. "What we need is another way out."

Behind us, I could hear the raspy calls of the draugr, closing in on us.

"There," said Ali suddenly.

She pointed to a dark alcove in the tunnel wall. Squinting, I could see the dim outline of a door. Painted above it, in faded letters, were the words EMERGENCY EXIT.

"I'd say this qualifies as an emergency."

The draugr were only a few yards away as I raced

towards the exit. If it was locked, I wouldn't have time to break it down.

I ran with all the strength I had. In only moments, the draugr would be upon us, ripping into our bodies with their wizened, leathery hands.

CHAPTER 29

ALI

Galin slammed through the door, then kicked it closed, pushing his enormous body against it. I clung to his neck as my eyes adjusted to the darkness of the side tunnel. Somehow, when I was close to him, I felt the warmth of the sun on my skin, smelled the scents of flowers. In the hollows of my mind, I even knew their names: lilac, honeysuckle, wild rose. It was like the world came alive again when I was close to him.

I felt his muscles shifting under me as he tensed, powerful arms encircling me. Draugr banged on the door, but Galin leaned against it, holding it shut.

"Ali." He was still catching his breath. "Do you think you can find something to jam the door? An old pipe, a piece of wood…."

I scanned the interior of the side tunnel, finding it unfortunately empty. "Nothing."

"Shit."

Behind him, the door shook with the pounding fists of draugr. My pulse raced out of control.

I looked up and down the escape tunnel, double checking

that I hadn't missed anything. A few motes of dust hung in the air above the ancient subway tile. This place had probably been empty since Ragnarok.

"Wait," I said, excitement rising in my voice. "Why don't you just create a portal? No one can see us use magic here."

Galin arched an eyebrow. "I don't love cheating."

Panic was making my heart race, and frustration crackled down my nerve endings. "What if we're about to be eaten by the undead, though? There's a time and place for honor, but this isn't it."

He sucked in a sharp breath. "I can make exceptions."

"Do you know where the Old State House is?"

"Probably best not to be seen stepping out of a portal right in front of the finish line." Galin paused for a moment. "I could get us to Faneuil Hall, just around the corner. Can you stand? I'll need my hands free to do the spell."

I wasn't sure if I could, but I had to try. Carefully, I unlinked my hands from Galin's neck and slid to the floor.

Putting weight on my leg sent fresh agony rocketing up my thigh, but I forced myself to do it. The draugr must have heard the movement, because on the other side of the exit door, they began to unleash ravenous screams. I could see Galin's shoulders and legs straining with effort as the undead slammed themselves into the metal.

I stared as he scribed glowing runes in the air. Moments later, the portal shimmered before us—a magical safety exit.

"Go." He nodded at it. "I'll be right behind you."

The draugr screamed, and the door shook behind Galin as if it were being repeatedly struck by a wrecking ball. I dove through the portal, landing on a snowy street. White hot pain lanced up my leg, but I still spun, waiting for Galin to arrive.

Instead, I stared in horror as the portal shimmered for a second, then disappeared with an electric crackle.

No. The scent of ozone washed over me, and my heart went still for a moment.

I could see exactly what he'd done, and I hated him for it. He had tricked me, again. He'd known that as soon as he moved his back from the door, the draugr would fling it open before he could make his way through the portal. They would tear him to pieces, and then they'd charge through the portal after me.

So, he'd simply closed it as soon as I'd passed through. He'd sacrificed himself for me.

Gods, this wasn't how I'd imagined any of this playing out.

I clenched my fists, my entire body trembling with shock, tears welling in my eyes. I should have seen what he was up to. I had no way to get to him right now, no way to help. At this point, all I could do was hope that he found a way out of there, despite the odds.

Worry electrified my mind.

Suddenly, I heard the distant shouts of elves. The Old State House must be close by.

I looked around, taking in my surroundings for the first time. Galin had dropped me in the shadow of an ancient statue. Though it was encrusted in ice and snow, it appeared to be a man with his arms crossed.

I looked away as a bestial howl rent the frigid air. Not elves this time. Draugr.

I stood, using the plinth for support, even as pain splintered my leg. I'd been stabbed before—Hel, I'd had my finger cut off—but this was different. Each step was like getting stabbed with the javelin all over again.

Gritting my teeth, I began to shuffle towards the Old State House. I could see it in the distance, now, an old red brick building with a large marble balcony. A group of elves stood in front, a mix of gasping runners and officials dressed in striped shirts.

As I shambled towards them, I tried to block out the pain, but I found my mind kept going back to Galin. I was trying to picture him fighting his way out of there, as if imagining it could make it happen.

It hadn't been that long since I'd planned to kill him myself. But now, I wasn't sure what I wanted. When I'd thought he'd betrayed me, it meant everything had been a lie. That he'd put up the wall to help us. That he'd help me free the Night Elves. Killing him had seemed imperative to freeing my people.

But if he hadn't sent the letter—if he'd spoken the truth— maybe he wasn't the monster I'd been raised to believe he was.

I believed him when he said the letter hadn't been his.

It seemed impossible, but he was trying to help me. He'd just sacrificed himself for me, hadn't he?

Already, guilt was eating at me. If I hadn't been there, slowing him down with my ravaged leg, he'd already be here. Safe. I swallowed hard, trying to stay focused.

When I was about twenty yards from the finish line, the elves began to cheer. I recognized Thyra and Ilvis. Even Bo was there.

I looked at Thyra as I shuffled through the snow. "How many?"

Thyra looked down State Street. "If you hurry, you'll be number one hundred and forty-six."

I could feel blood streaming down my leg under my leather pants.

Clenching my jaw, I pushed forward. Twenty, ten, five yards remained. I gasped for air like a dying fish, but my leg wouldn't keep going. I tumbled forward into the snow.

I was going to die here. Even before they had a chance to

execute me, the cold or the blood loss or the draugr would get me.

But Galin had sacrificed himself for me. I wouldn't let this chance go to waste.

Keep going, North Star.

The words emanated from somewhere deep in my brain. I pushed myself up on to my elbows. Army crawling the last three yards, I crossed the finish line at last.

I fell flat in the snow, breathing deeply. Thyra crouched by my side, and I groaned. I must have been moving on shattered bones.

"That was something else," said Thyra.

I grimaced again at the pain. "I don't fuck around."

I wanted to ask her if she'd seen Galin, if he'd managed to get here, but that was probably a bad idea. So, I pushed myself up, scanning the snow drifts for him.

I'm pretty sure that was when I blacked out, because the next thing I remember, I found myself propped against a rusted fire hydrant. I heard the elves cheering, saw them pointing down State Street. I concentrated, willing my eyes to focus. A single Vanir ran toward us.

"Last one!" shouted a Night Elf standing next to me.

"What do you mean?" My voice sounded distant and hollow. *How much blood have I lost, exactly?*

"We're at two hundred twenty-six elves! This is the final one! The rest will die in an execution." She clapped her hands.

Panic climbed up my throat, and I couldn't hold it in any longer. I looked up at the Night Elf. "Is Galin here?"

"The High Elf prince? I haven't seen him." She grinned. "Let's hope he got eaten by the draugr, right?"

Gripping the frozen fire hydrant, I pulled myself into a standing position. My heart ached. Yes, I'd spent my whole life wanting to kill Galin, but he'd also saved my life several times. And now, I felt safe around him. I hungered to learn everything about him. I felt my soul splintering.

Around me, the elves were focused on the single running Vanir, cheering him on. Then, after a few moments, I noticed their shouts rising ... they were cheering more wildly. I squinted at the track to see what had them so excited, and my breath caught.

Behind the Vanir, a second figure had appeared, running in great, galloping strides. A massive elf, shirtless, pants shredded and torn. His golden hair streamed behind him.

Somehow, Galin was alive.

The Vanir warrior glanced over his shoulder, then picked up his pace.

"Pity he's never going to catch up," said the Night Elf next to me. "Would have been an exciting finish."

The Vanir raced closer, Galin running behind. With his blood-soaked clothes and his blond hair flowing out behind him, he looked like a rampaging Viking. But I didn't think he could catch up. I forgot to breathe.

As he moved closer, I realized I recognized this particular Vanir. This was the very fucker who'd thrown the javelin into the air.

I was woozy with blood loss, but my mind became focused on the injustice of the situation. Galin had saved my life. The Vanir had tried to kill me. I needed to give Galin the upper hand, even if it was breaking the rules. Fuck the rules.

I took a step closer, my eyes locked on the Vanir. "Skalei."

The warrior was twenty yards out. I swayed, balancing on my good leg.

"Fly true," I whispered.

I flung the blade at the Vanir. He was running, but it slammed into his leg, just as I'd intended, slowing him down. With a scream of pain, he stumbled, clutching at his thigh. I'd been practicing my knife throwing, and it seemed like it was paying off.

I started to smile, but within moments, other Vanir were running for me. From behind, someone punched me hard in the skull. "Cheater!"

"Skalei," I turned, ready to fight with whatever strength was left in me.

But before I had to land a blow, a shadow spread over me —a massive elf, blocking the sun.

"Get back," growled Galin.

"The rules were clear!" shouted a Vanir. "In this trial, no thrown projectiles were allowed. She has forfeited her life."

I stood unsteadily, looking at the Vanir—the Regent himself, his hawk on his shoulder as always. He was pointing a finger at me.

"You want to lecture me on the rules?" Galin's voice was low and controlled, icy as the winds around us. "You who tried to have this very Night Elf murdered on the practice field."

"That was an accident—"

"It was not." Galin's hand shot out, and he grabbed the hawk.

I stared. What was he doing?

The bird screamed, thrashing in Galin's grasp. The Vanir were shouting, jostling each other. My leg screamed with pain, but I forced myself to remain upright.

Galin held the bird above his head and chanted in ancient Norse, and magic beamed around him. Screeching loudly, the bird bit and clawed at Galin's arm, and the air hummed with electricity.

The body of the hawk began to twist and shiver. Its feathers fell away, and Galin laid it down in the snow. Its skin peeled open, and slowly, a woman rose from the pile of feathers and skin. Her gray hair hung in a braid down the back of her gray wool dress. Her lip curled in a snarl, green eyes glaring. Shadows filled crevices in her gaunt, wrinkled face.

Galin pointed. "And here we have the person who directed the spear. A hamrammr. A shape shifter. In the form of a hawk, *she* tried to kill Ali."

The hag glared at Galin but didn't speak.

Thyra shoved her way into the crowd, eyes flashing, "Not just a hamrammr. A seidkona. A witch. The Vanir have been using magic to help them win all along."

"And so have you," hissed the seidkona. "Just now, as I was flying above Faneuil Hall, I saw the girl step from a portal. You've been cheating, too."

Thyra turned to me. "Is that true?"

I fell silent. *Shit.*

Thyra shook with anger, looking like she wanted to lunge through the snow to attack me.

The Vanir were starting to spread out now, slinking away. But King Gorm was moving closer, grinning. "So, both the Night Elves and the Vanir have been cheating."

Galin shrugged, shoving his hands into his pockets as snow fell on his bare chest. "Yes. And the High Elves, too. I created the portal."

"You what!" King Gorm's fluting voice blared off key.

Galin looked at the night sky. "We all cheated. Seems like it cancels out."

Silence fell over us.

Finally, Thyra spoke. "I find this acceptable."

"What about him?" said the Regent, pointing at the man I'd stabbed with Skalei. "If he hadn't been stabbed, he would have taken the last place. The prince cheated."

Galin cocked his head. "It seems to me that you've had an extra soldier on your side all along." He pointed to the feathers at the hamrammr's feet. "That would mean that instead of two hundred and twenty-five elves, two hundred and twenty-six elves may survive this contest. Rounding up, of course."

The Regent grunted. "Fine."

"Icy Hel, Galin," grumbled Gorm, his eyes blazing with rage. "Whose side are you on?"

CHAPTER 30

GALIN

An hour later, I was back in my quarters, and Ali was in the care of a Night Elf healer. Now, I understood exactly who'd come to my room that night before the melee—the hamrammr. The witch had visited me disguised as Ali, and she'd escaped by turning into a bird.

So much made sense now. When we'd visited Vanaheim, we hadn't seen any women. But they had been there, hidden. Witches in alternate forms.

I paced my room, trying to decide what to do.

Take me to the girl. Ganglati hadn't spoken for hours, and his voice startled me.

Why?

You told me you needed the girl to steal the wand.

I sighed aloud. *Fine, let me scribe a portal. I wanted to see her anyway.*

Quickly, I traced the rune in the air, and magic crackled over my skin as I stepped through into Ali's living room. Despite the darkness, I could smell her clean scent in here.

A few moments later, the door to her bedroom suddenly creaked open, and she stood in the doorway. She wore her leather outfit, and Skalei gleamed in her hand. She looked ready to kill me, which was oddly sexy.

"Oh." She slowly relaxed. "I thought you were a Vanir."

Someone banged on the door from the hallway outside and barked, "Who's there?" A male voice.

I went tense. We wouldn't be able to say much in front of whoever that was.

"Just me!" Ali called.

"I heard voices."

"Just talking to myself!" Under her breath, she hissed at me, "You *need* to leave now. Thyra's having me watched."

"Are you sure you're okay in there?" The door creaked open, and I slipped out of sight, into her bedroom.

"I said I was fine," I heard her say more firmly. "Don't make me annoyed."

"All right." The voice now sounded a little nervous. "Just doing my job."

As soon as I heard the door close, I stepped back into the room.

Ali's silver eyes flashed with worry. "You have to go."

"We both need to go. It'll be quick, I promise."

She let out a long sigh, and I caught the faintest hints of a smile at the corners of her mouth. "It's really hard to turn down someone who faced a horde of draugr to save your life."

"I was counting on that answer." I began to scribe the portal spell. In seconds, it hummed in front of me.

"Where are we going?"

"Somewhere we can talk privately."

I gestured at the portal, indicating she should step through. She flashed me a wry smile—like she wanted to be annoyed with me but couldn't—then stepped through. I followed close behind.

When I came through, she was standing with her back to

me, before a row of twenty-foot glass windows affording a spectacular view of Boston. Moonlight streamed over her silver hair, her form-fitting clothes. From where we stood, I could see both the frozen expanse of the Charles River and the marble walls of the Citadel.

Ali pressed her hands on the window, her breath clouding the glass. "This is amazing. Is this one of the old— What are they called again?" Her brow furrowed for a moment before she thought of the word. "Skyscrapers. But most of them are falling down." Her eyes flicked up to meet mine as she figured out where we were. "Except for the Prudential Tower." Ali breathed a low whistle. "Nice choice for a meeting spot."

I gestured at the room we were in. "Exactly right. We're on the very top floor of the Prudential Tower. A thousand years ago, this was a fancy restaurant. Rich humans would come here to eat expensive meals while they looked down on the city."

"Are we safe?" She nodded at the enormous windows that ringed around us. "Anyone could see in, right?"

"No one can make it up here on foot. The elevators broke hundreds of years ago, and the stairs are blocked by ice. The only way in is by moth or portal, but we're fifty-two stories up and the wind is fierce. Very few moths can fly high enough."

"Okay," said Ali, seemingly convinced by my explanation. "So what was it you wanted to tell me?"

Ganglati can you give me a hand?

Certainly, answered the shade.

Without speaking, I reached up and took off the Helm of Awe. I placed it on the floor in front of me, then took a step back.

Ali's eyebrows furrowed, then suddenly, her eyes widened. "You figured out a spell to remove the helm?"

"Temporarily, at times. You didn't notice when I helped you bury the body? I was able to walk around outside the Citadel then. Prior to that I had to get Gorm's permission to leave the Citadel."

"I didn't think of it," she said as she eyed the helm. "I guess traveling through portals is a bit disorienting for me. So, what kind of spell was it?"

I took a seat on top of one of the old restaurant tables. "I didn't use a spell. There were none strong enough to break the bond."

Ali cocked her head. There was something about the curiosity in her eyes that made her irresistible. "I don't understand. How did you do it?"

"I had to enlist help."

Ganglati, I said to the shade. *Reveal yourself.*

For a long moment, nothing happened. Then, I felt the shade move within me. Frigid and cold, he filled my veins with ice. Wisps of black vapor began to rise from my skin.

Across from me, Ali's eyes widened, and I heard her whisper for Skalei on instinct. "Galin. What did you do?"

"I struck a deal."

"You did *what?*"

My mouth opened, and Ganglati spoke through me in an icy voice. "It's so nice to see you again, little Night Elf."

Ali stared. I wanted to tell her not to worry, but Ganglati was in control of me now.

"You don't remember me?" said Ganglati. "Marroc's companion. We met in Helheim..."

Recognition sparked in her eyes. "The shade from Helheim."

"None other," said Ganglati.

"What did Galin agree to do for you?" said Ali suspiciously.

"Just a boon for my people. And I need your assistance," added the shade.

She gripped Skalei tighter. "Oh, Hel no. You won't even tell me what we're doing?"

"I've heard about your little problem with the Wyrd."

This got Ali's attention. "What do you mean?"

"Isn't it true that you want to break the bond that connects your souls?"

She crossed her arms, cocking her head. "Okay. What are you offering?"

"If you agree to help, I will take you to the Norns."

CHAPTER 31

ALI

I stared at Galin—or, rather, the shade that controlled him. He was rigid, his back ramrod-straight. Black mist rose from his skin, and his hair swirled about his head. His beautiful golden eyes had turned pitch black.

As terrifying as he appeared, he'd just made a pretty compelling offer. A chance to break the bond that bound my soul to Galin's.

"What do you want me to do?" I asked.

"I need you to steal Levateinn."

Again? I crossed my arms. "And how would I do that?"

"I thought you might know, since you're the expert thief and assassin."

"Well," I said, thinking quickly, "if I had Galin and his portal magic to help me, I might be able to do it. But how will I know you'll follow through on your end of the bargain?"

"A shade cannot lie."

True. "Okay, then I'll consider it. But I'm going to need to speak with Galin first. Can you return him?"

Slowly, Galin's eyes cleared, and the black vapor began to dissipate. He shuddered visibly. "That was unpleasant."

I stepped closer to him. "Tell me what you agreed to do for the shade. Wait," I said after a moment, "I think I know." I bit my lip, thinking back to the conversation he'd had with the shade in Helheim. The memory sparked in my mind. "He wants you to raise his queen, Hela, the goddess of the dead. Isn't that right? You said you could use Levateinn to bring her back, right?"

"Precisely."

This seemed like a terrible idea. "Do you really think it's a good idea to raise the dead goddess of the underworld? It seems like that might have consequences."

He gave a shrug. "Probably not, but making safe decisions isn't my strength."

"I'm starting to understand that." And yet, knowing Galin, I wondered if he had something else up his sleeve—a way out at the last moment—exactly like he'd done today with the portal. Getting out of insane situations clearly *was* his strong suit.

So how much confidence did I have in him to handle this?

With a shock, I realized that I was actually starting to trust him. But I'd keep this assessment to myself; if his plan was to turn the tables at the last second, he'd be hiding it from the shade.

I nodded. "Okay. You two want me to help you steal Levateinn. In exchange, he'll take me to the Norns, so I can become the mistress of my own fate." I shrugged. "I think it's a shit deal. There's no guarantee that the Norns will actually help me. And I believe *you*, but I'm not sure about this shade character." I nearly said *he seems a bit shady*, but then thought the pun would annoy me more than anyone else.

"Look." Galin scrubbed a hand over his jaw, his eyes gleaming. "There's more than just our bond at stake here. If I can get Levateinn, then I can take over as king of the High Elves. The first thing I'll do is break the wall that imprisons your people."

Now *that* was something worth considering. Hope beamed in my chest, a star growing brighter. At last, my dream was within my grasp. Maybe this was it? Maybe it *was* my destiny. "Do you promise?"

"Of course."

And there it was again—that strange realization that I trusted him. I smiled. "Okay. Now that you're free of the helm, can't you just open a portal? Should be a simple snatch-and-grab, right?"

"Unfortunately, no. King Gorm has thousands of runes protecting his quarters. The moment I open a portal in his room, it will be swarmed by guards."

"So, what are your thoughts?"

"I think we should try some human magic."

My forehead furrowed. Had he lost it? "Humans don't have any magic. That's why the High Elves have them completely subjugated. When Barthol and I were preparing to rob Silfarson's Bank, we had to live with them. They mean well, but many of them still refuse to accept Ragnarok. They insist that something called 'global cooling' is the cause of the endless winter."

"Human magicians do exist. Before Ragnarok, there was a subculture of humans who studied trickery. Specifically, sleight of hand. For example, they'd say they could make a coin disappear. But instead of actually doing magic, they'd distract the other human, and when they weren't looking, they'd hide the coin in their palm. It would only appear as if they'd done magic."

He slid his hand into his pocket and stepped closer to me. He flicked my hair off my shoulder, leaned in, and whispered in my ear in a deep, rich murmur, "Perhaps you could join me in my room later?" The sound of his voice and the closeness of his perfect face sent a hot thrill over my skin.

Then, from my other ear, he appeared to pull a silver coin. He held it up, grinning. "See? Human magic."

I fought to suppress a smile. Humans were lovely, simple-minded creatures. "Okay. This actually worked as a form of magic?"

A slow shrug. "In a way."

"So, this is a long way of you explaining that we need to distract King Gorm so that I can steal the wand."

"Exactly. I'll make a scene to distract him, and you steal it."

"When exactly do you want to do this burglary?" I asked.

He tossed the coin in the air, and it glinted as it spun. He caught it again. "Tomorrow night."

"That soon?"

"I've been thinking about how to do this for weeks. I have a plan." Galin fixed me with his gaze and drew in a deep breath.

I got the feeling, even before he spoke, that this would be another prime example of not taking the safest option.

CHAPTER 32

GALIN

That night, I fell into a deep, dreamless slumber from which I awoke fresh and rejuvenated. I dressed in a clean set of clothes and my favorite useless accessory: the Helm of Awe. It was important to keep up the illusion that Gorm was in control while Ali and I planned to steal Levateinn.

Once fully dressed, I walked down the stairs. Today, I arrived in the mead hall in time to snag some scrambled eggs, sausages, oatmeal, orange juice, and a mugful of piping hot coffee. As I sipped the coffee, I heard Revna call for me. Her voice was like sharp claws raking inside my skull.

I turned to see her sitting with Sune, dressed in a gold gown and waving her fingers at me. "Were you planning on dining with the lowlifes?"

"I wasn't. That's why I walked past your table."

When she replied, all the playfulness had disappeared from her voice. She went straight for the jugular: "Why did you betray us?"

I mentally calculated the best way to keep Ali alive. "Perhaps I have a plan, and perhaps the Night Elf is useful. How do you think I've survived this long?"

Revna's eyes slowly widened, and she grinned. "Oh, you naughty boy. So, she's an informant?"

"Tell me more," said Sune, leaning forward eagerly. "Have you seduced her for information? Mind if I have a go?"

Just as I was considering if this was the appropriate time to snap my brother's neck, a trumpet interrupted us, followed by the dulcet voice of the herald announcing the arrival of the king. King Gorm walked in slowly, looking tired. He'd survived the race, but not without considerable effort.

With a grim expression, he ambled over and sat next to Revna without looking at me.

"Daddy," said Revna in her most saccharine voice, "are you still upset with Galin?"

"I should have him executed for treason," he muttered. "But we can't afford to lose any more High Elves in the Winnowing. We're in last place." Only then did he slowly turn to look at me, speaking softly but otherwise not bothering to hide his rage. "Once this is over, perhaps we will find suitable accommodations for you in your former lodgings."

The dungeon, of course.

Revna sighed. "Father, that is a little excessive. Why don't *I* keep an eye on him?" She gave me a wink that put me right off my breakfast.

From the Vanir table, the Regent rose. "If I may have everyone's attention. Now that King Gorm is with us, I'd like to announce the final contest."

I scrubbed a hand over my jaw, staring at him. I'd expected him to continue with his announcement, but instead, he began waving his fingers in what I recognized as the runes of the portal spell.

An instant later, electricity crackled, and a dark void

bloomed a few feet to his right. It grew larger and larger, until it took up almost the entire aisle between the rows of tables. All around me elves began to scream. Then, I saw why: a beast of hair and muscle, nearly as tall as a horse, charged into the hall, snorting and grunting loudly.

"Eofor!" shouted the Regent. "Eofor, sit."

And just like that, a monstrous boar sat in the great mead hall of the High Elves. It was covered in bristly black hair and smelled terrible, like the contents of a sewer that had fermented in the hot sun. When its head turned to look in my direction, I saw beady eyes set behind a pair of ivory tusks nearly the length of my forearm.

A giant fucking boar.

All around me, elves were shouting and jumping out of the way as the boar began to snuffle and snort. A dark purple tongue slid out from between the tusks, and it began to snake plates of pancakes, bowls of oatmeal, even—I grimaced—pieces of bacon into its maw.

"Quiet! Quiet!" shouted the Regent at the terrified elves. "We don't want to upset him. This is Eofor, the largest of the royal hogs."

King Gorm had risen, still clutching his cutlery. "Why in Hel did you bring this revolting creature into my hall?"

"I'm terribly sorry, King Gorm," said the Regent, gently patting the giant boar on its cheek. "When Eofor is well fed, he's really a fine fellow and very well-behaved, but unfortunately, he digests his food very fast and gets hungry again. All this breakfast will come out the other end soon enough."

The boar leaned forward, snuffling loudly as he tried to reach a plate of sausages.

"Which is why we will be hosting the final contest this evening. We will be releasing Eofor and five of his brothers and sisters onto the grounds of Mount Auburn Cemetery. I haven't fed Eofor's siblings for nearly two weeks, and even after he gobbles up these crumbs, he will still be quite hungry. The goal of our contest is simple: don't leave the confines of the cemetery, and don't get eaten. When half of the remaining are dead—one hundred and thirteen elves—the contest ends."

The hall fell silent, interrupted only by the sound of Eofor's chewing.

Revna raised her hand. "Will we be able to bring weapons?"

"Of course, anything you like. But I should warn you that the hide of a Vanaheim boar is exceptionally thick. I don't think you'll succeed in piercing it." The Regent paused for a second. "But that does remind me. We won't be allowing any magic. None whatsoever."

CHAPTER 33

ALI

Alone, I crouched in the back of a tomb. Ancient marble blocks surrounded me, encrusted in sheets of dirty ice. A moldering skeleton lay in a nearby alcove. I hugged myself tight, teeth chattering, still trying to block out the pain in my leg. And trying to block out my memory of what had just happened.

Two of the Shadow Lords lay dead. I'd barely escaped as the boar had charged Thyra and Ilvis, goring them to death. The images kept flickering in my mind—the ivory tusk piercing Thyra's chest, Ilvis trying to save her. Blood on the snow, the Shadow Lords screaming. I'd felt like the world had dropped out from under my feet as I'd watched the boar tear Ilvis to pieces. Two of my leaders were dead, and I hadn't been able to stop it.

I thought I'd been here for an hour, maybe—biding my time in Mount Auburn Cemetery while waiting for another boar to appear.

Situated in Boston's suburbs, Mount Auburn Cemetery had remained untouched for hundreds of years. Over the past hour, the setting sun had cast lengthening, eerie shadows on tombstones frozen in ice. Now, moonlight streamed onto the icy floor of the tomb. I tried not to think of Ilvis's screams...

The plan had been for all the Night Elves to stick together, but that had all gone to shit when the first boar attacked. We'd been ambushed out in the open. The Shadow Lords had been the first in the line of attack.

The Regent had been right; the boar hides were virtually impenetrable. Even Skalei hadn't been able to do much more than scratch it.

And now, I found myself alone in a tomb, surrounded by broken marble and skeletons. It was dark and cave-like, which I liked, but it was also a dead end. If a boar found me inside, I'd be cornered. Still, my bad leg was a major impediment to moving around, and I didn't want to be caught limping around in the snow.

The scream of a boar ripped through the air, making my muscles tense. It was a caterwauling cry that prickled the hair on my arms. I gripped Skalei tighter, ready to fight if I had to.

As I steadied my breath, a shadow fell over the entrance of the tomb, and my heart skipped a beat. "Ali?"

Galin. Quietly, I crept to the doorway of the tomb and peeked out. Galin stood on the path not twenty feet away, looking for me.

"Over here," I whispered.

He spun around to face me, then hurried over. "Thank the gods you're still okay."

He'd been disarmed. "Where's your sword?" I asked.

"Broke it on a boar. Those things have hides of steel."

"Thyra and Ilvis are dead. I couldn't—" A boar screamed again, and my stomach flipped. My Night Elf eyes strained, staring into the darkness, until I saw movement along the crest of the hillside opposite us. The silhouette of an enormous creature, its heavy footfalls shaking the ground.

My stomach clenched as a new pair of shadows came running along the path, closer to us. The boar was charging two people, and it took me a moment to realize who they were—Revna and Sune. The dumbasses' shrieking was drawing the attention of the boar, and they were rushing down the hill for our hiding spot.

"Galin! I know you're near! I can feel your power. You have to help us!" Revna cried. To my horror, she and Sune were running right for our tomb. My future tomb, if she didn't fuck off.

From the top of the ridge, the boar bellowed, charging for Revna as she led it to us. I heard Galin growl as she and Sune ran inside.

The entire tomb shook as the boar slammed into the entrance. Bits of ice and marble rained down on us from the ceiling. I coughed as rock-dust filled the interior.

The boar howled and screamed like a banshee. Its massive head filled the doorframe, tusks jutting into the empty space. Grunting and twisting its shoulders, it tried desperately to squeeze inside, but its body was too big. It snorted loudly, filling the tiny room with the stench of its breath. By now, I was pressed up against the wall, Galin standing in front of me like a shield.

Then, the boar stepped back and disappeared into the wintery darkness.

The sound of heavy breathing filled the tomb, each of us gasping for breath.

"Did it leave?" asked Sune.

Before I could say, "I doubt it," the boar barreled into the marble doorway like a wrecking ball. Again, the rock shook and dust rained down on us. This stupid beast wasn't going to stop until it got us.

"We can't stay in here," I said quickly.

Revna stared at me like I was a complete idiot. "If we go outside, the boar will kill us."

I pointed to the ceiling, which had cracked open from the force of the attack. Great chunks of marble threatened to rain down on us. "The roof is going to collapse. If we stay, we'll be buried alive. Not to mention that that thing is absolutely strong enough to break in here and eat us."

The boar had disappeared into the darkness, quiet again. In the moonlight, I could just about make out the shape of the beast turning around, steam rising from its back and snout. In seconds, it would be charging us again, and we'd be buried under marble.

I had to do something. As a Night Elf, I'd have the best chance of seeing the boar in the darkness of the tomb. I recalled Skalei and crouched, readying myself, praying for the roof to hold.

The boar charged again, smashing itself into the entrance like a freight train. Dust rained down, and stone shifted above us, but the ceiling didn't collapse. As the boar thrashed in the doorway, I leapt forward, trying to plunge Skalei into its cheek. Despite the ferocity of my attack, I hardly made a dent. Boar hide, it turned out, was the one thing a shadow blade couldn't slice.

The boar screamed, so loud and close it felt like it was ripping my brain open. Then, its tongue lashed out, twisting around my ankle like the coils of a snake.

Galin lunged toward me, grabbing for my arm. But the boar was too fast, ripping me out of the tomb, dragging me into the wintery night. Snow filled my mouth and eyes. Frantically, I wiped it away only to smell the stench of the boar and to see the blood of the elves it had already eaten dripping from the ends of its tusks. I knew that in moments, it would begin to eat me alive.

I struggled against the prehensile tongue to no avail. Galin charged from the entrance of the tomb, trying to distract the boar, to offer himself instead, but the creature wasn't interested in him.

I had to do something. The boar's tongue was tight around my ankle, purple and glistening. Then, a thought came to me: maybe the tongue wasn't as tough as the creature's hide.

"Skalei!" In one swift movement, I slashed. It was like a hot knife through butter.

Blood sprayed the snow. I'd hacked part of its tongue right off. I was free.

I tried to stand, but my injured leg buckled, and I fell.

The boar squealed again, a broken gurgling sound this time. Then, it fixed me with its beady black eyes and lunged for me, trying to gore me with its tusks. I barely rolled out of the way. Grunting and snorting, it spun on massive hooves, and I scrambled away on hands and knees, pain racing up my thigh.

The boar charged, its breath clouding in the frigid air, blood and lather dripping from its chin.

Out of the corner of my eye, a shadow moved. Galin was racing toward the beast, something long and pale flashing in his hand. He leapt, silent as a ghost, and thrust his weapon at the boar's face. The boar's screeches rent the air, and it staggered back. Two more steps, and then it toppled like a felled tree. A human femur quivered in its eye.

Galin turned to me, but my gaze was on a new boar—massive, with black fur and a tank-like body. Eofor stared right at us from the top of the hill.

He stood for a long moment, snorting steam. Then, he threw his head back and squealed—a terrible sound like jagged bones scraping on stone. An instant later, he was answered by another, then another. And now, a chorus of squeals and grunts rose from the woods behind him.

"Ali!" Galin held out his hand to me and pulled me up. "We can't stay here."

Again, Eofor's enraged cry rent the night air. I doubted I'd be able to outrun him.

CHAPTER 34

GALIN

The cold air burned my lungs as I raced with Sune and Revna through the snow of Mount Auburn Cemetery. Ali was managing to hold her own, keeping up with our frantic pace, even with her injury. I broke trail through six inches of snow. Ali just had to hold out a bit longer. I knew a safe place.

A boar squealed suddenly into the night. They were closing in on us.

"Where are we going?" whispered Revna sharply.

"Shhh … don't let them hear us."

Revna was quiet for a few seconds before she spoke again. "Galin, we can't run forever. We should find somewhere to make a stand."

The boar screamed again, cutting her off. It couldn't be more than a hundred yards away.

"There," I whispered sharply, pointing up.

Silhouetted against the night sky was Washington Tower. Nearly five stories tall, it had been constructed as a lookout atop the tallest hill in the cemetery. It would be the perfect refuge, built from solid marble, the stairwell far too narrow for the boars to climb. We just had to get there.

I led the way up the hillside, weaving between trunks of ancient trees encased in ice. Half way up, I looked back down into the valley below. The enormous shapes of the boars were closing in on us, charging.

When we reached the summit, I let Sune and Revna go on ahead, as I held out my hand to Ali. She gripped it hard, and I pulled her up. She crouched beside me, gasping for breath and grimacing. Obviously in considerable pain.

I slid my arm around her waist and helped her move toward the entrance. She was limping, leaning into me. As the boars started charging up the hill for us, I scooped her up and carried her into the tower stairwell.

I heard tusks rake the stone, but we were safe for now. Holding her tight to me, I started climbing the spiral staircase. She rested her head on my chest, and my pulse raced at the contact.

Just a little farther and we could rest.

At last, I reached the top. I eased Ali from my arms, and she slid down my body, sparking a surge of warmth throughout my muscles.

We stepped onto the top of the tower, a small circular roof ringed by tooth-like stone crenellations. From below, the boars grunted with frustration, trying to hammer the tower with their shoulders and tusks. I peered over the edge. Four of the beasts paced around the base of the tower like sharks circling a life raft.

Still, there was no way they could possibly reach us. We were safe.

Revna leaned against the railing, next to Sune. "You made it," she said to me, then narrowed her eyes at Ali. "You trailed blood all the way here, you know."

My chest tightened as I saw the blood streaming from Ali's leg. She desperately needed medical care.

Suddenly, a shadow passed over us—a High Elf riding a moth. One of the judges. "One hundred and fourteen remain. The Night Elves have lost badly!" she shouted down to us.

"One left," said Revna, turning to look at me. "One more elf dies, and this is all over." She refocused on Ali and drew a dagger. "The Night Elves are losing anyway. She dies no matter what. Those were the terms, right? If the Night Elves lose the Winnowing, they all die."

"Looks like we can win this," said Sune.

"Don't you dare," I growled.

"Skalei," whispered Ali.

Revna lunged with a knife, but Ali parried the strike. Fast as lightning, Ali lunged, slashing Revna in the face with the tip of her blade. Blood sprayed across the white marble of the tower.

At first, I thought Ali had killed her, but then my sister moaned. Slowly, she sat up, clutching her face in her hands. Ali had carved a gash diagonally across her face.

With a snarl, Sune slammed his fist into the side of Ali's head, so hard I heard the crack echoing out over Boston. Before she had a chance to recover, he was holding his own knife to her throat. "You dare come after my sister?"

Ali was out cold, limp in my brother's arms.

I wasn't going to stand by and watch them kill Ali, even if it meant I would give away the truth about the Helm, that I'd found a way around it.

Help me kill them, Ganglati.

Certainly, he whispered.

Sune brought his blade up, ready to bring it down into Ali's throat.

Ice water filled my veins, and I lost control of my body. With an inhuman scream, I ripped him away from her.

I threw Sune over the side. For a final instant, I saw him suspended in midair, pale hair flying, eyes wide as saucers, before he disappeared out of sight.

Then came the jubilant squeals of the boars, and the shouts from the judges that the hunt was over.

CHAPTER 35

ALI

I paced the length of my room, back and forth, back and forth. Even after rewrapping the bandage, my leg ached. My thoughts whirled wildly between three things.

The first was the Winnowing. The final tallies had been thirty-nine High Elves, thirty-nine Vanir, and twelve Night Elves remaining. The Vanir and the High Elves had tied so far.

Worst of all, the Night Elves had lost. The addition of the Vanir to the Winnowing had disrupted our plans completely. I thought if they hadn't turned up, we would have won. We could have freed ourselves from the caverns, lived in the sunlight, found a new source of food. We could have stopped the starvation.

Grief carved me open. The Vanir boar had trampled our plans into the dirt.

Now, we'd been eliminated from the Winnowing. Either the High Elves or the Vanir would have dominion over us. If the High Elves won, they would march their soldiers into the Shadow Caverns in the next few days. Then they would kill every last one of my brethren. I had to hope now that the

Vanir would win, and that they would be merciful. But they didn't exactly seem like the merciful type. I still didn't understand why they'd entered the Winnowing to begin with.

Then, there was Galin.

He'd killed his own brother to save me, and I had no idea what sort of punishment he'd face. But it seemed our plans to find the wand were now in ruins.

After he'd thrown Sune off the tower, High Elves on moths descended on us. Revna immediately told them what happened. Galin had been marched out of the tower in manacles.

I turned Skalei over in my hand, then threw her at the door to my room.

Thunk.

She quivered in the wood. I was getting even better at the knife throwing, though I wasn't sure what good it did me now.

I swallowed hard. With Sune's death, the trial had ended. The High Elf moth-riders took the little princess to safety, leaving me up there. I had to find my way back to the Night Elves. I didn't exactly get a hero's welcome. I was now considered a traitor again.

When I'd reached them, they stood in a half circle, their weapons pointed at my heart. Bo, the lanky fucker, thought he'd make himself a new Shadow Lord. He revealed how I'd blackmailed him. He told them Galin and I were secret lovers, and that I'd pressed a knife to his throat and threatened to kill him if he told anyone.

He told the Night Elves I'd abandoned them to join the High Elves, that it was my fault we lost.

That sealed my predicament. I was supposed to disappear for good. So, I'd packed my bags and waited.

I recalled Skalei, then threw her at my door again. *Thunk.*

By consensus, I'd been banished to Midgard.

I glanced at the door, hoping Galin would visit a final time. When I went into hiding in Boston, absolutely no one would be able to find me. Not even him.

It was after 1 a.m. Disappointment slid through my bones. I thought that if he could have, he'd have created a portal by now to find me.

I pulled open the door to my room just a crack and looked out into the dark hallway. I wondered if they'd taken Galin to the dungeons or simply locked him in his room.

I moved into the hallway, keeping to the shadows. What I needed was an informant.

I heard a cough, and ducked into a shadowy alcove just as a guard walked by. He passed, and I slipped up behind him and pressed Skalei to his jugular.

"Feel that steel?" I whispered in his ear. "It's cold, right? I'll warm it with your blood if you don't answer my questions. Now, nod to show that you understand me."

I felt him shaking as he nodded.

"Good. Now, where is Galin? Answer me quietly."

The guard gave me directions in a tremulous whisper.

When he'd finished, I wrapped an arm round his throat, squeezing to deprive him of just enough oxygen. I wasn't going to kill him, but I wanted him out for a while. He struggled in vain for a minute or so before going limp, and I dragged his unconscious body into a room, out of the way.

Then, quietly as possible, I followed the guard's directions to Galin's quarters.

I'd expected Galin's door to be locked, but instead, it was wide open. That didn't seem promising.

"Skalei," I whispered.

Moving quietly, I crept inside. His room was a disaster. His bed torn apart, his pillowcases cut open, books strewn everywhere. There was no sign of the prince.

Quietly, I shut the door behind me and started searching

C.N. CRAWFORD

the room, but I just found more destruction. I began to poke around, flipping over books, looking under the blankets. What had they been searching for? Some sorcery thing, probably.

I stepped into the trashed bathroom next. What I saw stopped me in my tracks.

With black charcoal, someone had written *F-word A* on the mirror.

What in Hel?

My eyes lingered on the mirror. What exactly did *F-word A* mean? Why not just write *Fuck*?

But maybe it wasn't some vandal guard who'd written that. What if it had been written by Galin?

What if it was a message?

F-word A. I looked closer at the A. There was something more beyond it, a part of another letter. A sort of vertical smear. Which would make the full phrase, as written, *F-word Al.*

It could be a message to me, and Galin had been interrupted while writing. *F-word Ali.* That had to be what he'd been trying to write.

What in Hel does that mean? Fuck Ali? I couldn't see him censoring his own mirror-swears if he really wanted to express rage.

"F-word Ali," I said under my breath. "F-word Ali."

I paced around Galin's quarters, muttering to myself. What was he trying to tell me? A warning, maybe?

I tried to envision what had happened. Someone had come to his room, and he'd known he only had seconds to send a message. He'd grabbed charcoal and written on the mirror. *F-word Ali*—only he'd been cut short.

Maybe his message hadn't been a warning; maybe it was some sort of instruction.

F-word. That's what he wanted me to know. What F-word could he have been referring to? *Fuck* was out. Friend? Frog? Fluffy?

But even as my mind raced through the possibilities, the answer was crystalizing in my subconscious. Galin had used a special magic word to hide his home in Cambridge. It had started with *F*.

I racked my brain trying to remember what it was. It seemed like ages had passed since I'd been cornered by the horde of draugr on the broken fire escape. I remembered how Galin—or Marroc, as I knew him then, back when he was cursed—returned, parting the undead with his makeshift torch.

He had left me in the path of danger, but he'd returned to me. Just like he always did.

I concentrated, trying to remember the word I'd used to reveal his hidden home. *Finland? Farthing? Furniture?* No, it had been in Old Norse.

I squeezed my eyes shut, as if that might help squeeze the word out of the depths of my mind. Now, I remembered how he'd used the burning femur to scratch the word into the frozen dirt while warding off the bloodthirsty draugr.

It started with an F, then an I, then an N.

He'd protected me. Kept me safe. And he'd smelled of smoke and sage.

There was another N.

I had it—all the letters in a neat little row in my mind.

"Finnask!" I nearly shouted.

At first, I thought nothing had happened. Then, I turned around. Where the remains of his desk had stood was now a neatly ordered workbench. A row of jarred herbs, stacks of vellum and parchment, a big stack of leather-bound spell books.

I crossed to it to get a better look. In the center was a small scrap of paper.

Dear Ali,

I'm sorry, but I haven't much time before they come back for me. Do not try to help me. It is too dangerous. If you want to save your people, now is the time. Gorm won't be in his quarters tonight. Sneak in, steal the wand. Use it to free your people. Any sorcerer should be able to help you do it.

Forever yours,
Galin

My heart sped up, my chest unclenching a little. So perhaps there was hope, after all? Maybe all was not lost. Not yet.

I stuffed the note in my pocket and whispered, "Finnask," again to hide the workbench. He was right. I still had to do whatever I could to save my people, even if we'd lost the Winnowing.

I was turning to leave when I heard voices in the hallway. I glanced at the door and remembered that the lock had been smashed.

Revna's voice floated through the stone hallway. "The tunnel-rat is missing, but at least Galin is going to get what he deserves. Fratricide. It's the worst sort of murder, except maybe regicide. And it was practically that, too! The monster was killing anyone with a claim to the throne."

I dove behind the bed just as the door to Galin's room swung open and High Elf guards began to pour into the room.

CHAPTER 36

GALIN

I stood bare-chested on the dais, peering over into the Well of Wyrd. They'd taken my coat and shirt. A soldier pointed a wand at my heart. The obsidian lid that normally capped the well had been removed, and I stood inches from the depths. If I made one false move, the hex would slam me back into the void, and I'd plummet all the way to the roots of Yggdrasill.

In the night sky, the moon shone brightly. Nearly full.

High Elves crowded the amphitheater seats on the roof of the Citadel to watch my execution. It wasn't every day the crown prince was accused of treason. Of murdering his brother. And while I'd planned to destroy my family all along so that I could assume the throne, this hadn't been part of the plan.

I'd done what I'd had to do to keep Ali safe.

Perhaps there was still time for me to find a way out. Ganglati, at least, had gone quiet in my mind.

A trumpet sounded, and my father strode onto the dais, not far from me.

I peered down at the Well of Wyrd. This was where it had

all begun—only, this time, Ali wouldn't be here. This time, they intended for me to plunge to my death alone.

Gorm looked like he wanted to gut me himself. Even his fear had burned away with rage. He knew he was next. "I should throw you in without a trial."

"The law says otherwise."

"Silence," he snapped, and turned away from me to face the crowd. "I have asked you all to come here to pass judgement. My youngest son, Prince Sune, is dead. My eldest son, Galin, is accused of killing him."

A hush passed over the crowd. For many of them, this was the first time they'd heard of this.

I looked around the amphitheater. There was no sign of my sister. "Where is the witness?" I asked.

"Revna!" bellowed the king.

His voice echoed in the wintery air. Silence greeted him. The frozen wind whipped over me.

It began with hushed murmurs, then movement in the back of the crowd. Then more voices. At last, Revna appeared at the top of the steps. She wore a long, flowing gown of lace and fur. A bright red slash ran diagonally down her face where Ali had cut her.

She raised her arms. "Father, I am here," she said, loud enough that every elf in the amphitheater could hear her. "I am here to tell the truth about what Galin did."

Then, slowly, making a grand show of it, she began to walk down the steps. By the time she reached the dais, the crowd was murmuring with excitement.

Revna stopped next to my father, then pointed her index finger at me. "This is the man who murdered my brother. But after careful consideration, I request mercy for him. The Night Elf cast a love spell on him. He is helplessly in her thrall."

The High Elves cheered wildly.

Only when they quieted was I able to speak. "And how exactly was I able to murder my brother?"

Revna looked at me like I was a complete idiot. "You threw him off the top of Washington Tower."

"Right, but *how* could I have done that?"

She shook her head in disgust. "Is this going to be your defense? Parroting questions back to me? I saw you do it— you picked him up by the collar and tossed him over the side."

"But how could I have attacked him, dear sister, when I wear the Helm of Awe?"

Revna was trembling with rage. "I don't know how in Hel you did it! I know what I saw. I want you in chains, brother. In chains and under my command."

I didn't want to entertain what disturbing fantasies she might have in mind.

"Clearly, the helm is broken," the king's voice boomed. "You've used your magic."

"Absurd!" I returned, pretending to be shocked. "It's unbreakable."

King Gorm's eyes narrowed. "Prove it. You swore an oath to me, that you would remain loyal. As my loyal subject, I need you to prove your fealty."

"How would you like me to do that?"

The king reached into his belt and withdrew a long dagger. Gold plated, of course. He tossed the dagger at my feet. "I order you to cut off the ring finger on your left hand."

Gritting my teeth, I reached down and picked up the dagger. This was ... not ideal. And of course he would choose something twisted.

"If you don't do it, I'll have you thrown into the well!" yelled King Gorm. And there it was again—that fear. He was terrified of what I'd do without the helm, if it didn't work.

I could ask Ganglati to take over now, to kill him. But this wasn't the time. Not with all the wands pointed at me, ready to slam me into the well if I failed to prove my fealty.

I gripped the blade tightly. It was just a finger.

A heavy silence fell over the amphitheater. "As you wish," I gripped the blade and pressed it against the first knuckle of my left-hand ring finger. With a sharp movement, I cut it off.

The pain was unimaginable, taking my breath away, but I held up my hand and blood pumped from the bloody stump.

The crowd roared, and that was when I knew I'd won.

"You see," I shouted, gripping my wrist, "I have proven my fealty undoubtedly. I'm afraid my sister was confused."

Quietly, under my breath, I whispered a spell to start healing the severed finger.

"This is all the fault of the Night Elf," said Revna. "The sorceress. Bring her out. We will have her confess her trickery."

An icy trickle of fear began to fill my veins. I didn't want Ali anywhere near this.

A guard appeared at the top of the amphitheater. Next to him, gagged and bound, was Ali. He shoved her down the stairs, and she stumbled.

"She was a witness," said Revna. "Let's hear what *she* has to say. She's a dark sorceress who has enchanted my brother. It is she who must die."

I felt a strange sort of déjà vu as Ali stumbled onto the dais. She couldn't speak, but her eyes locked on mine.

Revna ripped off the gag. "Tell them what happened. What *really* happened."

"You killed Sune. I saw it." said Ali slowly. "You lied."

Now *that* was interesting.

"No!" Revna clutched her hair, looking like she might rip it out. "You ruined everything. I knew you would ruin everything. Why are you even still alive? They were supposed to have killed you!"

Ali's nose wrinkled. "Who?"

"The Shadow Lords! I sent a letter, telling them exactly what you'd done. That you betrayed your own people. That you helped Galin. Why did they let you live? You are a traitor to your own kind."

Ali's silver eyes flashed bright. Her silver hair whirled around her head in the icy winds. "*You* were the one who had me sent to prison? *You* wrote that stupid letter?"

Revna pointed to her face. "Do you think I regret it, after what you've done to me? You've been exiled now, haven't you? You are no longer under the Night Elves' protection, and your kind doesn't get a trial. Time's up, *Astrid*."

Every one of my muscles was now tightly coiled as I got ready to defend Ali.

King Gorm fixed his eyes on me. "Galin, now you must truly prove your fealty. It is time for you to kill the Night Elf. Fail, and you will be thrown into the well."

I stood there, staring at him as it became completely obvious to everyone in the amphitheater that I'd been lying about my complete loyalty. And it also became clear to me that I was about to plummet into the well if I didn't come up with something fast.

"I order you to kill her!" the king shouted. "You promised loyalty to me, correct?"

"I will not," I murmured.

Revna's eyes flashed in the moonlight. "She *has* enchanted him. But don't kill him, Father, please. I want him in a prison. I want him in chains."

King Gorm looked to the crowd. "Our subjects came here for an execution."

"No!" Revna screamed. "We can keep him locked up. An iron cuff around his throat, locked to the wall."

A heavy silence fell over the amphitheater, and my fingers

twitched where my sword should be. With my finger still healing, I wasn't sure I could fight even if I'd had a sword.

King Gorm raised a hand. "Kill the Night Elf first. I have not yet decided what to do with the prince, but I may feed him to my troll. Porgor has been so hungry of late."

The king flicked his fingers. Instantly a soldier fired a hex. I dove in front of Ali, and the spell slammed into my legs. There was no slowing my momentum. I tipped over into the Well of Wyrd.

CHAPTER 37

ALI

I felt like someone had just carved my heart out. I pushed away from the soldier who'd been holding me and ran to the edge of the well, watching Galin disappear into the darkness. Silent horror chilled my soul. Frozen by a stunning spell, I knew without a doubt there was no way he could have survived the fall.

The Night Elves had lost the Winnowing. The High Elves would remain in power and my people would be exterminated.

And now, I'd lost Galin, too. I felt like my heart was shattering into pieces.

Back when I was imprisoned in the Audr Mines, I'd spent every waking moment dreaming of his death. I was sure that was my fate—I would end his life, bring down the wall. It would be the answer to everything.

But I'd just watched him fall to his death. I felt numb. I no longer thought his death would free my people, that it was the answer to anything. It was as if my chest had been carved open, hollowed out. I was empty.

I felt like I'd fallen with him, plummeting into a void.

It took me a few moments to realize it wasn't *just* Galin's loss that had left me feeling ripped apart. With his death, the bond between our souls had broken. I was completely unmoored, plunging through the dark.

But I couldn't lose myself in grief right now. I had to be sharp and clear as a star in the sky, or I'd be dead, too.

Revna stared at the well, looking nearly as devastated as I was. As I watched her, a strange thought occurred to me. Had she actually *loved* her brother?

She whirled to look at me, tears gleaming in her eyes. Her golden hair caught in the icy wind. "This was your fault. He was going to be my husband, just like the ancient bloodlines. Two royals, joined in a perfect union."

"He *what*?" Gorm spluttered.

"Don't act shocked, Father. You know we have different fathers." With tears streaming down her face, Revna stalked towards me.

"Skalei," I whispered, readying myself for a fight. But it would be damn hard to fight here when soldiers were pointing their wands at me.

I was inches from the lip of the well, and my senses raced into overdrive. High Elves surrounded me. Above me, I heard the wingbeats of hovering moths, the buzzing of spells. There had to be dozens of wands pointed right at me, far too many for me to dodge. All King Gorm had to do was say the word and I was dead.

Revna took another step towards me.

"Come any closer and you'll feel my blade between your ribs," I said, but I knew the threat was empty.

And yet, maybe if I goaded her, I could gain the upper hand.

"I'm sorry your brother didn't love you," I said bitterly. "I know for a fact that he loathed you."

Her jaw tightened. "Put down that blade, bitch, or I'll have you shot."

I dropped Skalei onto the dark stone. I'd follow along. I'd draw her closer.

Tears streamed down Revna's pale cheeks. "Now put that gag back in your mouth."

So, she was clever enough to know that I'd simply call Skalei back if I could. I pulled the gag into my mouth anyway.

Revna took another step closer. Her face was a mask of pain and rage. Like me, she appeared unarmed, but I knew there was no way that was actually the case. She'd have a blade close at hand.

It took a second for me to glimpse the hilt of the dagger in her sleeve. She thought she was being sneaky, didn't she?

When she was within striking distance, steel flashed in her hand.

I caught her wrist, driving the dagger away. In one fluid motion, I slipped behind her and pulled her close to me, pressing the dagger against her stomach. Any movement would cut her open.

I wanted to kill her, but I could use her life as leverage. She was the only remaining heir to the High Elf empire. The perfect human shield.

Gorm bellowed, "Let her go!"

I was still gagged, so I could only shake my head no.

And that was where I fucked up. Because Revna wasn't a normal person who thought in normal ways. Revna was driven by some sort of insanity. She wanted to win at all costs.

She ripped herself out of my grasp, and the dagger carved into her gut. Even as she shrieked in agony, she elbowed me so hard in the chest that I fell backward.

Everything moved in slow motion. I tried to balance, but

there was no ground under my feet, only the depths of the Well of Wyrd yawning beneath me.

For a split second, my fingers clawed at the lip—then I was in free fall.

CHAPTER 38

ALI

Cold air rushed past my face as I plummeted into the darkness of the Well of Wyrd. The dark granite of the well flew by, just a few feet from me. I had thirty, twenty seconds before my body shattered on the roots of Yggdrasill.

I was about to die. Tumbling and spinning. Faster and faster. Panic ripped my mind open.

I was about to become a fresh corpse on King Gorm's bone pile. Galin and I would be companions in death.

Air rushed in my ears, and with it came a sound echoing in the depths. "Aiiiiiiieeeee…"

Strange … I'd remembered the Well of Wyrd as a quiet place, but there it was again. A noise, louder this time. A voice.

I flipped around, flinging my arms out to steady myself. Far below me, there was movement in the darkness, and a faint purple glow. A dark form clung to the rock.

I understood the noise now. Not a scream, but my name drawn out.

"Aaallliiiii!"

Sacred gods. Galin was alive?

With one hand, he clung to the wall of the cave. With the other, he reached out for me. I extended my arm, but too late. Our fingers brushed, and then he was gone.

I kept falling. Sleek rock rushed past me, a gray blur only a foot away. And something else, black and sinewy, twisting in the cracks. Dark tendrils like the bodies of snakes. The roots of Yggdrasill.

I doubted they'd hold my weight, but I grabbed one anyway. My fingers wrapped around the wood. My arm jerked, and I slammed into the granite wall. The air rushed out of my lungs; my arm nearly wrenched free of its socket. Yet somehow, my fingers remained locked on the root.

I hung for a long minute, trying to catch my breath.

Then I looked up. My Night Elf eyes could pierce the darkness, but still, I couldn't see much—gray stone and the World Tree's roots twisting along the wall of the well, forming a ladder.

Galin was up there, somewhere.

I began to climb the roots. My shoulder and chest throbbed painfully, but I was able to make it work. Slowly, I made my way up the side of the well.

Above me, a violet glow began to illuminate the shaft of the well. It came from a hollow in the rock, a sort of cave. And standing in front, silhouetted against the violet glow, the muscular body of a High Elf I'd come to know very well. He waited for me on a narrow ledge.

My heart started beating faster, harder, hope lighting me up. "Galin?"

"Ali? Is that you?"

"Who else would have been thrown into the well?" I climbed towards the light. There were fewer roots here, and I had to find handholds in the rock itself. My forearms burned with fatigue.

When I was a few feet below him, Galin pulled me up

onto the narrow ledge, then wrapped his strong arms around me, practically crushing me into his steely chest. Warmth radiated from his body over mine.

I looked into his golden eyes, not quite believing he was real. "I thought you were dead. But I guess it's not the first time you survived a fall into the Well of Wyrd."

"Are you hurt?" he murmured.

I shifted away from him, rolling my shoulders cautiously. There was some soreness, but no serious pain. "A little banged up, but nothing major. Did you know your sister is in love with you?"

He shuddered visibly. "I'm not sure *love* describes it. She wants to control me. I'm a thing that she wants."

I wondered if Revna had managed to survive. "I, um … stabbed her in the stomach."

His eyes widened. "Did she live?"

"I don't know."

"There's something very wrong with her."

"I realize that now. How's your hand?"

He held it up, and I was shocked to find that his finger was still there, albeit mangled and with a jagged red scar at the bottom. "I whispered a spell to heal it, but the spell only worked partway. As soon as I climbed up here, it stopped working."

I frowned. "Wait, so you could have healed my finger all along?"

He shook his head. "It had to happen right away."

Behind him, violet light bloomed from an opening in the rock. I had the vaguest recollection of seeing something like this when we had first descended the well on the moth's back.

"There's something in there." I stood on the narrow ledge, gripping a strand of Yggdrasill's root for balance.

I moved in quietly, keeping to the shadows. Who knew

what else lived in the well—I distinctly remembered how I'd nearly been eaten by a Nokk in a subterranean lake. All sorts of creatures could be lurking in the darkness. Quietly, I tiptoed into the glowing mouth of the cave.

I could feel my eyes widen as I surveyed the interior. It was full of glowing purple crystals, like the inside of a giant geode. And these were not any crystals, but vergr crystals. More than I'd ever seen before. If I'd found a cache like this when I'd worked in the Audr Mines, I'd have been immediately granted my freedom.

"Hello, hello, hello," said Galin, his eyes wide. He stepped inside the cave by my side.

"Galin," I said excitedly. "Do you know what this means? With this many crystals, we could outfit every soldier in the Night Elf army with a vergr crystal. Can you imagine that? We'd be unstoppable."

Galin ran his fingers along the crystals. "The magic in this place is like nothing I've seen before. Simply amazing." He turned back to me, and the violet light illuminated his golden eyes, his finely sculpted cheekbones. The cave went about twenty feet in, then ended abruptly in a curved dead end. But there was so much crystal in here, it could change everything for the Night Elves—even after we lost the Winnowing.

Maybe I was the North Star after all.

Galin flashed me a sly smile. "Alright, where should we go?"

Someplace no one will find us. "The Prudential Tower?"

Galin nodded and began to trace the air. I'd seen him do it enough times now that I recognized the portal spell.

As he finished, I waited for the static pop of the portal materializing, but it never came.

"Hmm…" Galin frowned. "I must have missed a rune."

Quickly, he scribed the spell a second time. Again, nothing happened.

Galin moved back to the entrance of the cave and tried again. This time, for a brief second, a portal appeared before it disappeared with a hiss of static. He tried again and again. Nothing.

He turned to me, frowning. "Something is interfering with my magic." He held up his hand. "Just like the spell was interrupted when arrived here. My magic isn't working down here."

Oh, *no.* "Try something else," I said desperately.

Quickly, Galin scribed *kaun*, but the fire only appeared for an instant before disappearing. Galin's eyes widened suddenly.

"What is it?"

Galin didn't answer. Instead he reached up and gently touched the Helm of Awe. Then he took it off.

"Did you just—"I began.

Galin nodded. "The spell is broken.I can't even hear Ganglati."

He held the helm in his hand a moment longer, then with a hard flick of his wrist he threw it into the well.

Watching it drop into the depths gave me an idea. "Maybe we can use one of the crystals. Do you know how to enchant one?"

Galin shook his head. "Even if I could, how would we get it out of here? There's no way to get it to the surface. The roots stop soon, the walls smooth out. And if we dropped it down the well, it would shatter ..."

"And if we teleported to it, we'd simply reappear in a thousand pieces," I finished grimly.

I sat down on the edge of the ledge, my legs swinging over the abyss. Quietly, Galin sat next to me. For a long time, we looked out into the darkness of the well without speaking.

"Let me see your finger again," I finally said.

He held it out, and I grimaced. It had started bleeding again.

I tore off one of my shirt sleeves. "Here, let me bind it for you." I took Galin's hand in my lap, then picked up my sleeve. "This is going to hurt."

"I was dead for a thousand years. I'll withstand a bit of your shirt."

"There you go."

"Thank you." His voice was quiet and subdued.

I nodded and looked out into the darkness again, sighing. I couldn't stop myself from wondering what would happen next. With the Winnowing tied, who would win? The Vanir, or the High Elves—and what would become of my people?

Sadness shattered me, and my head fell into my hands. "We're trapped here, aren't we?"

CHAPTER 39

ALI

Grief-stricken, I peered over the edge. The vines I'd been climbing wouldn't take us down far enough to get to the bottom. Above and below them was sheer rockface, slick as obsidian. So, it was just us and the rocks.

I tried not to imagine how our death would go. We would become severely dehydrated within days. We'd starve and possibly consider eating each other.

"I'm not going to eat you," I muttered.

"That's a relief." Galin stared into the darkness. "This wasn't in my vision."

"What vision?"

"My vision of my fate. I saw myself as king."

"Of course you did."

He shot me a sharp look. "My visions don't lie."

"Right. Fate. Wyrd. You are deeply committed." I peered over at him skeptically. "Was I in this vision of yours? You said our souls are entwined."

He shook his head. "No. That perplexed me. You were not there with me in my kingdom. Which is wrong, obviously."

"I thought your visions don't lie."

His jaw tightened. "I am admittedly confused."

"The story of fate that my mother told was one where I killed you. So, if you really believe in fate, maybe we're not supposed to be lovers. Maybe our souls are entwined for an altogether different reason."

"And why would you kill me now?" he asked.

"For sustenance." It was a grim joke, and neither of us laughed.

Galin had gone completely silent, so quiet it was starting to worry me. "Maybe you're right," he said quietly, finally.

"What?"

"A thousand years ago, I devoted my life to the gods. Everything I did was to honor them."

"What about the women? I heard you had legions of women following you around. Desperate for your attention."

He shrugged. "The women were nice. But if it weren't for the gods, my life would have been empty. The deaths on the battlefields, the magic. When I died, I lost all those memories. I lost all meaning. For a thousand years, I was a shell of a person. I only started to feel alive again when I met you, even if I was still a lich. It was like I could feel my heart beating again, even if it wasn't supposed to."

I felt my own heart speeding up, warmth blooming in my chest. "Yeah?"

"And then my soul returned to me. With the power of Loki's wand, I had blood flowing in my veins. And my memories came back for the first time in a thousand years. But with that came the horrible realization that the gods were dead. Nothing meant anything anymore ... except you. Maybe Wyrd no longer means anything. Maybe fate was wrong, or stopped mattering after the gods died. But I do have you, and you're my light in the darkness. Where I once sacrificed to the gods, I'll now sacrifice to you."

I felt my breath catch at his words. "Wait, what? I'm not

like the gods. I'm nothing like a god. Haven't you been paying attention? I'm deeply flawed. You've heard me sing, haven't you?"

"You gave me a reason to be alive. Which means you're the reason I have to die again."

Fear snapped through my brain, and I grabbed his bicep. "What are you talking about?"

A muscle twitched in his jaw. "If I become a lich again, I can survive the fall."

I shook my head. "Nope. You're not going to kill yourself. I won't let you lose your soul again. Not until—"

He met my gaze, his golden eyes piercing me. "Until what?"

"I don't know. Just give it time. Maybe something will happen. Maybe a moth will fly down here. You'll forget everything again. You might not remember who I am. And what if we can't get Loki's wand back?"

Galin stood on the ledge, then crossed back into the cave. "Stay where you are, Ali. You don't need to see this."

"No!" I jumped up as he crossed into the glowing violet cavern. Galin picked up a sharp chunk of vergr crystal from the cave floor—a jagged shard, like a blade. He held it above his wrist.

My heart skipped a beat. I wasn't going to stand by and watch this happen.

I'd spent years honing my fighting skills, and none honing my diplomacy skills. If I couldn't talk him out of it, I'd fight him out of it.

I ran for him, grabbing the wrist of the hand that held the crystal. His grip was pure steel, so I slammed a punch into his cheek. His face snapped back, and the feral look he gave me nearly made my heart skip a beat. He growled, pulling his wrist out of my grasp.

"You're not doing this, Galin." I ran at him again, knocking him back hard into the stone.

He slammed back into the wall. The force was enough to shake the rock. This time, the shard clattered to the ground, and I snatched it up. I had the shard. A small victory, but a victory nonetheless.

But Galin was charging for me, and he pushed me back against the wall. He gripped my wrist, pinning it against the cold stone. His strength was, quite frankly, ridiculous.

His gaze flicked to the shard. "I'm going to need that, my Night Elf. I have a plan."

"Your plan is stupid."

His face was close to mine, mouth inches away. Runes glowed on his powerful chest. The corner of his lip twitched. "Did you really think you could beat The Sword of the Gods in a fight?"

"Do you *really* call yourself that? You have got to be kidding me." I slammed a knee into his gut, and he staggered back.

I still had the shard of vergr crystal.

I didn't know exactly what I was doing here, only that I'd managed *very* successfully to distract him from trying to kill himself. And frankly, I could fight him all day. He didn't get hurt easily. It was exhilarating, and maybe I liked having his body pressed against mine …

Snarling, I leapt at him. But he was leaping for me, too. We collided hard. But with his greater weight, the impact pushed me backward. Together, we slammed into the wall. At the last moment, he managed to cup his hand behind me to soften the blow against the stone, stopping my back from cracking against it. His other hand was just below my ass, gripping me tight. Just like at the battlefield, my legs were wrapped around his waist.

I breathed deeply, my pulse racing out of control as I

RUINED KING

looked up at him. He peered into my eyes, the gaze sliding right into my very soul.

He seemed to have forgotten all about the crystal blade now, and his lips grazed my neck. The sensation sent wild heat racing through my body. After the fierceness of our little tussle, the kiss was so excruciatingly gentle. With every brush of his lips, I felt desire building in me, a wild need.

"Galin," I whispered.

In response, he kissed my throat, and I arched my neck. Now, my hips were moving against him.

"A kiss before I have to go," he whispered huskily.

"You're not going."

I wrapped my arms around his neck, pulling his mouth to mine. It was a desperate kiss, wild and hungry. The kiss deepened, and I could feel it, then. Our souls entwined.

I wasn't sure if I'd ever before felt so alive. Every inch of my skin felt sensitive, ready for his touch.

While he held me against the wall, I reached down and began untying the straps of my armor. Then, I unwrapped my legs from him and unclasped my bra, revealing my breasts while he stared. He pulled off my trousers, then my underwear, his fingers skimming over my skin in a way that made my heart race. The cool air of the well kissed my skin, and I flashed him a seductive smile.

He stared at me for a moment, his smile sensual. "You are so beautiful."

Then, a fierce expression overtook his features. I reached out, undoing his trousers. As I did, he kissed me desperately, hungrily, like he'd find the meaning of life through our kiss.

When he was as naked as I was, I threaded my fingers into his hair, kissing him back, ready for more.

"You're perfect," he whispered.

For a moment, I pulled away from the kiss, and I gazed into his golden eyes. My pulse raced even faster as I read his desire there, his need for me. And something I hadn't yet noticed in his expression before. Normally so fierce—I saw a hint of vulnerability. He *needed* me, and he seemed to be searching my eyes for answers.

He slid his hands under my ass, and lifted me against the wall again. With his mouth on my throat, he left a trail of searing kisses along my skin, moving down toward my breasts. He was touching me, caressing me where I needed to feel him. As he held me up, I rocked my hips into him, against his hardness. I arched my back. A wild ache had built within me, and I found myself desperate with need. "Come on, Galin."

He thrust into me, holding me up against the vergr crystals. Pleasure rocketed through me in waves, and I was soaring. I could feel his heart beating against mine, powerful and alive. His thrusts strengthened, fingers tightening around me.

To think I'd once wanted to stop that heart. To think I could fight what the Norns had written for me. His existence had a magnetic pull to me, and I would keep him alive at all costs.

I moved with him, crying out with the ecstasy of my release, and he moaned into my neck. I felt shockwaves shuddering through my body, and I leaned on his chest, catching my breath. I stared into his pale eyes, determined to keep him safe no matter what.

CHAPTER 40

GALIN

Ali lay next to me, asleep. It was cold in the cave, and she'd curled up close for warmth. While she slept, I was thinking of becoming a lich again.

I couldn't bear to part with her just yet, but I could see what the future held. We would only have a few days before we succumbed to dehydration. Did I really want our last moments together to be unquenchable thirst and delirium?

Unless there was something else I could do ...

Covering Ali in my shirt, I slipped back to the mouth of the cave. Quietly, I peered into the well. It was just as it was before. Dark above and below, sheer rockface, illuminated only by the faint purplish glow from behind me.

I heard footfalls, then Ali jerked my arm back. "Don't even think about it." She pulled me back from the ledge. "Not yet." She heaved a sigh as she sat down next to me.

I sighed. "I'll give it time."

Ali slid her arm through mine and leaned into me. "Can you explain to me why the king hates the Night Elves so much?"

"He said he blamed you all for Ragnarok, but I wasn't sure

if he believed it. Having an enemy worked well for him politically at the time. You were the perfect scapegoat to blame for the suffering of the High Elves after they left Elfheim." A beating sound high above pulled my attention away. Fear, anticipation made my muscles tense. "Do you hear that? Is it—"

"Moths," breathed Ali, her silver eyes gleaming with excitement. She started pulling me into the cave. "Probably High Elves here to make sure we're dead. I'd rather they not spot us."

I stepped back, but still peered out to watch. Slowly, the dark forms of giant moths began to glide out of the darkness above us. Four, five, six of them. They circled, and I could see the unmistakable shapes of riders clinging to their backs.

"Call your dagger," I whispered. "There are riders. Do you think you can take one out?"

"Skalei." Ali paused, then cursed and shook her head. "Skalei won't come."

Not even Ali's shadow magic worked down here. I was going to have to do this the hard way.

"Stay here," I whispered, then I stepped up to the mouth of the cave, calling out, "Hello!"

The riders turned, facing me, but something wasn't right. They moved stiffly, bodies jerking awkwardly to each beat of the moths' wings. They balanced like they'd never been on a moth before. These were not the king's moth-riders.

One descended, crossing into the violet glow of the cave. I caught a glimpse of black hair and green eyes. These riders were Vanir. I searched around for a weapon, snatching up the crystal shard just as a moth dropped level with us.

"Prince Galin?" asked the Vanir, leveling a crossbow at my chest. At that moment, I realized I recognized him as the Regent.

"Is the Night Elf with you?" the Regent asked, then peered over my shoulder. "I see her there in the shadows."

I heard Ali take a step closer, sidling up behind me.

"How did you know we were down here?" I asked.

"Everyone in the Citadel knows what King Gorm did to you."

"And why are you here?" I barked.

Perched on the moth, he shrugged. "We came to collect your bodies. But since you're alive, you will come with us."

I took a step closer. "Why?"

He shook his head. "That is not for me to say at this moment. I can only give you my oath that Ali will be safe with us."

I frowned. This was completely perplexing. He had given his oath that Ali would be safe, but on multiple occasions Vanir had tried to kill her. "Give us a moth, and we'll follow you."

The Regent shook his head again. "No. I will take Ali with me."

"And we're just supposed to trust you?"

The Regent nodded, the faintest hint of a smile on his face. "I don't think you have any other option."

My mouth went dry. He wasn't wrong about that. I shot a nervous look at Ali. This could be a trap of some sort. But if it was, perhaps it would be easier to get out of than this pit of death.

* * *

A MINUTE LATER, I was sitting astride a moth's back, gripping its fur tight. The Vanir warrior in front of me awkwardly jerked the reins, and we nearly slammed into the wall of the well. The poor guy could probably break a stallion in his sleep, but equine skills simply didn't translate into moth riding.

At least I'd managed to grab the crystal shard before we left. Hopefully I would survive this ride.

"You need to relax," I said sharply. "Let the moth do the flying."

The warrior grunted, ignoring me.

"Look, why don't I take the—"

Before I could finish, the Vanir had leaned too far left. Now thoroughly unbalanced, the moth flipped upside down. I gripped tight with my thighs. The Vanir screamed, clutching at the insect's antenna.

Gods help me.

"Grab it round the head!" I shouted, but too late. The moth thrashed, and the Vanir was thrown clear. In an instant, he'd disappeared into the darkness.

Above me, I could hear the other Vanir shouting, but I didn't have time to listen. If I didn't immediately get control of the insect, it'd break its wings and crash into the wall.

After a few harrowing seconds, I managed to grab hold of one of the moth's antennae in a solid grip.

I swung the moth right side up, adrenaline pumping, breathing hard. They would think I killed the Vanir, so I held up my hands, signaling I wasn't a threat.

"He lost control!" I shouted.

But there was no one there to respond. My voice echoed in the darkness of the well. I was alone. No moths circled above me. No chitinous wings beat the air.

"Ali?" I shouted, spurring the moth higher.

Only echoes answered me.

"Ali?" I shouted again, panic flickering in my chest.

I was about to scribe *kaun* for light when I smelled ozone, sensed the static in the air. A portal had been cast.

I could guess where they'd taken her. I raised my hand to

scribe a portal to the Vanir's quarters in the Citadel. If anything happened to her, the Vanir would feel my wrath.

Before I could finish my portal, cold magic raced down my arm, freezing it in place.

We stay here, Ganglati hissed. *We need the wand.*

I froze. Ganglati was right. If I were going to take on the entire Vanir realm, and if I were going to help stop the slaughter of the Night Elves, I would need Loki's wand. I'd be taking on not one, but two kingdoms, by myself. And that required serious magic indeed.

My heart slammed against my ribs. I just needed to make sure I got it *fast,* before anything happened to her.

CHAPTER 41

GALIN

*I*t was late afternoon and I sat, alone, in the derelict Prudential Tower. Closing my eyes, I allowed my soul to slip away, into the astral plane. I needed to check on Ali—to see where the Vanir had taken her.

I'd never ascended to the astral plane from the top of the tower. At first, I saw only darkness, but as my psychic eye focused, I saw thousands of tiny, shimmering souls spread out below me. Now, I just had to find Ali's.

I began by swooping out towards the Citadel. Immediately, I spotted King Gorm and Revna. Gorm's soul glowed brightly, but Revna's seemed off, flickering slightly. I was surprised at how little I felt for her and Sune, but maybe that thousand years I'd spent in the dungeon with no heartbeat while they taunted me had soured me on them.

As I floated closer, I saw that Revna's light had faded, as if her soul was slipping out of Midgard. I'd only seen that a few times, and only when people were near death. That was Ali's doing.

But I could see no sign of Ali here.

"Where is she?" I muttered.

I hadn't expected an answer, but Ganglati spoke. *Well, she's not in Midgard. And she hasn't been executed, or she would be in Helheim with me.*

My chest unclenched. It hadn't occurred to me that Ganglati would be able to tell me she was alive. "So, she's in Vanaheim."

That would be my interpretation.

"Okay. My father is alive, but my sister is injured." I slid back into my body, my muscles flexing.

That is also what I see. The shade paused. *So, we steal the wand now?*

"Now or never," I said quietly.

Rising, I assessed my gear. I had an old dagger and a pair of thick leather pants. Not exactly a full suit of armor, but it would have to do.

I drew in a deep breath as I prepared to draw a portal. My plan was a good one, but that didn't mean it would be easy to pull off.

I will help you, said Ganglati, his voice once again a whisper in my subconscious. Though that wasn't particularly reassuring.

I drew the portal and stepped through, the magic crackling over my skin.

I appeared in the hall before King Gorm's quarters. The usual pair of guards stood on either side of the towering golden doors.

I stalked closer to them, a cold anger chilling my blood. I wanted vengeance, now. "I am here to speak with the king."

The guards stared, mouths open in shock. They looked pale as milk, like they'd seen a ghost. "We thought you died," one of them stammered.

"Did you honestly think the Well of Wyrd can kill me?" I narrowed my eyes.

He was shaking as he answered. "No one visits the king without prior approval."

"Are you sure you want to annoy me? I seem to survive no matter what you people do to me. Do you think the same is true for Gorm? In a battle between us, which one do you think will end up as king? You might want to start reconsidering your loyalty."

The guard on the right's eyes twitched, and he glanced to the other for help.

"You don't have to let me inside," I offered. "Just go in and tell him that I'm here."

The guard on the right nodded, then pushed open the doors and disappeared. Only one guard remained.

In two strides, I was at his side. I slammed my fist so hard into his head that it snapped back against the door with a crack. Unconscious, he began to fall, but I caught him. The main doors were locked with runes, and his hands were the keys to opening them. Grabbing one of his wrists, I pressed his palm against the door. It swung open.

The curtains were drawn, and it was dark in the main room. But behind a door to my right, I could hear my father talking to the other guard.

I pushed open the door and entered to find my father and the guard staring at me. An enormous stained-glass window loomed over Gorm, depicting him dressed as the god Freyr with a boar and an enormous sword.

I crossed to his oak table and plucked an apple from his fruit bowl, taking a bite. The apple was perfectly sweet and tangy, and it made my mouth water. I wanted to throw him off guard.

"As it happens," I began casually, "the rumors of my demise turned out to be wildly exaggerated. It would appear that I'm still standing."

"Galin," stammered my father. "I know you'll understand that I did what I had to do."

I shrugged. "Sure. Moving swiftly along. Where is it?"

"What?" Gorm looked confused.

"The wand. Levateinn. I'll be taking it with me."

"I don't have it." I'd expected my father to lie, perhaps tell me that he'd had the wand locked away somewhere outside the Citadel. But that wasn't why I'd asked him.

He was a dreadful liar, always had been. As he spoke, his eyes told me everything I needed to know. The wand was where he looked first—in the bedside table five feet to his left.

I dropped the apple and lunged.

My father began screaming: "Porgor! Porgor! Porgor! I have a meal for you! A fine meal!"

I ripped open the top drawer. Sitting at the bottom, wrapped in silk and shimmering with silver light, was Levateinn.

I snatched it up and began to raise it. But before I could cast a spell, the floor below me exploded, throwing me across the room.

"*Blrooooooahhh!*"

Porgor, my father's troll, had entered the arena.

CHAPTER 42

GALIN

The troll landed in front of me, and the floor shook like an earthquake was ripping the world apart. I stumbled to my knees as the ground swayed. Great chunks of plaster dropped from the ceiling. Porgor bellowed again, the sound loud enough to make my eardrums tremble.

I rushed to my feet, but not fast enough. Porgor grabbed my arms, each of his hands like a steel vice.

From across the room, my father screamed, "Kill him! Kill him! Kill him!"

Porgor's grip tightened. His granite fingers began to crush my forearms, but I still had Levateinn. The only problem was the wand wasn't pointed at him. He was twisting my arm, leaving the wand pointed at the wall, which was no use at all. If I destroyed the wall, the whole ceiling would come down.

My father grinned, enjoying what he perceived as a victory. "I have to give you credit, Galin, you came close. But to beat me, you need to be focused on the real world. You always had your mind on runes and spells. The gods. You were better as a lich than as an elf, because at least you'd forgotten the gods."

The troll squeezed. I had a plan; I just needed to goad him. "The Norns have decreed that I will rule the High Elves, Gorm. I'll bury you in the snow."

Gorm was shaking with rage now. "You don't deserve a death at my hand. A troll is too good for you. I should feed you to the dogs."

The troll was pressing harder. I was barely able to speak, "Is that what you said to my mother? Before you had her murdered for choosing a better lover?"

Gorm's grin disappeared in an instant. "Do not speak of your mother in my presence."

"Still embarrassed that she found you boring?"

Gorm was nearly screaming with rage now. "Bring him to me!"

Porgor grunted and began to shuffle forward. Beneath his massive feet, the floor shook like the skin of a drum. My father's eyes bored into me, filled with pure, unadulterated rage. He'd drawn a dagger from his belt.

I flashed him a wry smile. "You can't imagine how happy it makes me that you are not my real father."

Under the light of the stained glass, Gorm's eyes burned with anger.

Porgor took another thumping step directly in front of the towering window. The tip of Levateinn was aimed straight at the glass now.

I shouted, "*Kaun!*" and a great gout of flame rushed across the room, melting his sacrilegious image.

The breaking glass revealed the snowy landscape outside, eddies of snow blowing wildly. I stared out at the eternal winter. The ruins of the city spread out beneath us, tiny buildings buried in snow, brick homes with icy roofs, the husks of the frozen skyscrapers.

In the distance, the shining ice of the Charles River reflected the last amber rays of the sun. My salvation.

"*Blrooooo*—!" Porgor's howl was cut short when he noticed the light. He stopped moving, his beady eyes staring out the window. Caught in the glow of the setting sun, the skin over his knuckles began to harden into solid stone.

With a grunt of pain, the troll released me. The floor shook as he stepped back into the shadows.

"Porgor!" shouted Gorm, panic rising. "I *order* you to get back here and kill him!"

Porgor grunted a final time, his eyes flashing red hot as he looked at my father. Then, with a final step, he disappeared into the hole he'd made in the floor.

Gorm howled with rage and lunged for me, his dagger aimed at my chest, but I easily dodged out of the way. He sailed past me, losing his balance. I pointed the wand at his chest.

As he picked himself up, his eyes locked on Levateinn, "You wouldn't dare. This is regicide."

"But I will be the new king." I raised Levateinn and shouted, "*Yr!*"

The bolt of magic struck him in the chest, slamming him backward. Smoke rose from his torso, and the scent of burnt flesh curled around me.

CHAPTER 43

ALI

The Regent was leading me to the Vanir temple, but I still didn't know why he'd saved me. And I didn't know what the fuck had happened to Galin. Just before we'd gone through the portal, I thought he was about to slam into a wall. I worried for him, but at this point, I knew one of his most defining characteristics: getting out of near-death situations at the last second. I tried to convince myself that he was probably fine. He'd gotten out of worse, hadn't he?

As for me? I had a strong sense that I was being led to my death.

This seemed less like a rescue and more like an abduction. After all, I'd killed their Emperor. What was the Vanir punishment for regicide? Being hanged, drawn and quartered, slowly tortured to death? Pierced with a thousand arrows? Drowned in boar's blood? I had no idea. It would probably be excruciating, and dread stole my breath.

The temple rose before me, and fear made my heart skip a beat.

We entered, and I stared around, panic crackling up my spine. When I'd visited it before, it was largely empty, a sandstone mausoleum with a giant hall full of golden light and not much else. But now, it was packed with Vanir warriors standing in rows. Hundreds of elves, each wielding a curved saber. Each of them here to watch me die—I was now certain of it.

The Regent led me to the front of the temple, then turned to face his men. His hawk—the hamrammr—flew down to rest on his shoulder. He spoke to me and to his men. "In our kingdom, bloodline does not matter, only strength—power. Only the strongest of our warriors can become our leader. If you kill the Emperor, that is the first step to becoming the new ruler. If you then withstand three attempts on your life, you become the rightful heir to our realm. We have sent assassins twice. Our witch sent the spear at you. You withstood all three trials. You are the North Star we have been waiting for."

"The what?" I stammered.

"The North Star," he repeated. "Our savior, as it is written in our chronicles. The one we have been awaiting. You will lead us to greatness."

I felt as if the world was tilting beneath my feet. The North Star?

There was a puff of feathers and then the seidkona stood before me, her eyes blazing with anger. "Not yet. I only sent one assassin."

I shook my head, trying to get my bearings. She was lying, and even though I felt dazed by this turn of events, I knew I had to master control of the situation. This was life or death. "You sent an assassin to my room, personally directed a spear at my leg, and lets not forget the mob of Vanir that attacked me during the footrace. This is why you joined the Winnowing, isn't it?" I said, finally putting it all together. "You wanted to kill me yourself so that *you* could claim the throne?"

The Regent glared at the seidkona. "That is enough. I kept

very close track of the assassination attempts. There were three. Three trials, as required. Our North Star is with us."

The seidkona sputtered, "But the Night Elf hasn't been thoroughly tested. She cannot lead us. We must amend the rules in this situation."

My legs felt weak, shaking. But this moment was a crossroads, a test in its own right. I could either crumble, or I could seize control—the way a true leader would. If I could control the Vanir, I could save the Night Elves in the caverns.

The Vanir and the High Elves were still deadlocked in a tie. If the Vanir could still win the final tiebreaker—with me at the helm—freedom would be ours at last. My mind was whirling a million miles a minute, but I had to get control, immediately.

Swallowing hard, I raised myself to my full height. I schooled my features into a serene expression. "Do not speak to your Empress that way, witch," I said firmly. "And do not doubt me. I stabbed your Emperor in the heart. He was dead before he began to burn. You have sent assassins after me twice, and you personally tried to kill me on the practice field. All three attempts failed."

A hush fell over the hall.

The seidkona's eyes widened. "But she is a Night Elf!"

"The law is clear," said the Regent. "And we will not amend it. She killed the Emperor and withstood three trials. The Night Elf is heir to the realm."

Hope swelled within my chest like a sea breeze filling a sail.

In a rush, the Vanir warriors surrounded me, shouting my name and banging their swords on their shields. The noise was deafening, but I had to focus. We still had a Winnowing to win.

"Stop!" I said.

Immediately, they fell silent.

"You accept me as your Empress?" I asked.

"Yes!" the warriors shouted in unison.

"We are at your service!" someone shouted.

"Our lives are yours," said another.

I locked eyes with the Regent. I knew the seidkona wasn't about to let this go. "We must speak in private. In an hour. And between now and then, I want you to send warriors to look for Galin."

* * *

An hour later, I was sitting in the Emperor's chambers dressed in fresh clothes: black leather pants and a dark silver shirt.

I sat at an oak table by a window that overlooked rolling fields. On the table before me was wine, hot venison stew, and a salad of tomatoes and dandelion greens. I was starving, but before I could bring myself to eat, I needed answers.

"What is the news of Galin?" I asked the Regent, my heart hammering.

The Regent shook his head. "He has not been found. At your request, one of our warriors flew to the bottom of the well. He retrieved the body of one of our men, but that is all. Galin, it seems, did not fall to his death."

I loosed a sigh. *Good.* Now, my stomach started rumbling, and I dug into the rich meal. Gods, it was amazing. "And you locked the seidkona away, right?"

"As you commanded, Empress," said the Regent. "But these are not the most pressing matters."

I beg to differ.

He shook his head again. "We need to make your position as Empress official. We must arrange for a coronation."

"Why?"

"It will ensure your safety. The Vanir will not touch you once you are crowned."

I felt blindsided, my mind still on the Winnowing. I didn't feel like an empress—still like a soldier who had a final battle ahead of me. "Can we make this coronation fast? After the ceremony is over, we must prepare for our final trial with the High Elves. We must win the Winnowing. Can we go down to the throne room and do this coronation now?"

"There is no throne room, Empress. Your power comes from the land—from Vanaheim's mountains, plains, and forests. You must ask them personally that they recognize you as Empress. Then, you will be secure."

I sighed. "How exactly does that happen?"

* * *

Eight great stones ringed us. Nearly as tall as the treetops, they towered over the grass of the meadow. Beyond them, the verdant forest stretched out over rolling hills. It had rained recently, and I could smell the fresh pine and wet earth. Clouds hung low above us, misty and gray. The air was completely still. It felt like the world was holding its breath. Waiting for what was to come next.

Meanwhile, impatience was rising within me, my mind still on the Citadel.

The Regent stood before me, his cloak pulled tight. He held a simple wooden crown in his hand. With a slight nod, he indicated that I should kneel. Then, holding the crown above me, he spoke in a clear voice.

"Astrid, daughter of Volundar. With this crown, you become Empress of the Vanir. You take up the mantle once worn by our gods: Freyja, Freyr, and Njord."

The Regent placed the crown on my head. And at that moment, I felt a surge of power within me, like a light piercing the darkness. I forgot about the Citadel, the Winnowing, about the caverns. Warmth and light beamed down my body, filling my limbs, my bones. I knew it then, down to my marrow. Strange as it seemed, this *was* my destiny. I felt myself melding with the land—the lush green forests, the undulating hills and the golden sunlight. The spirits of Vanaheim were calling to me, whispering around me, filling me with joy.

When I opened my eyes again, the memory of the Night Elves rushed back into me. And I started to understand. I would lead them here. *This* could be our home. As Night Elves, we would live in the real light of the moon and stars, under an open night sky. I would join our two kingdoms.

"Now, rise, Empress of Vanaheim, and meet your people."

I stood slowly, but I saw no people, just the ringstones. What people? For some reason, my heart was pounding in my chest. Not exactly fear, but something close to it. I stole a glance at the Regent. He was still as a statue.

Then, I saw it: a low fog creeping out from between the trees. It drifted over the grass of the meadow, slipping like water between the stones. I shivered as mist wound around my ankles.

The mist thickened, and the light dimmed. Cold, damp air slid over my skin.

The crown felt heavy on my head.

Around me, the colors of the forest faded; the smell of the pines vanished. The only thing I could see was the ring of stones looming above me. Under my feet, the soft grasses turned hard.

A footstep crunched on gravel.

"Empress." It was a new voice, cracked and brittle.

From between the stones stepped an ancient crone. She was tall and bony, with white hair that fell in thin wisps to her shoulders. She wore a ragged gray dress, and a small rucksack was slung over her shoulder. Slowly, she shuffled towards me, towering over me.

"Are you a seidkona?" I asked, nerves sparking.

"My name is long forgotten." The crone fixed me with a pair of shining blue eyes.

I stiffened. They were the exact same color Galin's had been when he'd been a lich.

The old woman smiled. "You have nothing to fear from me, dear. I am here to help you. That's what you want, isn't it? You are the new leader of the Vanir, the first Empress in a thousand years. You'll need all the help you can get, correct?"

Cautiously, I asked, "What are you offering?"

The crone's smile widened. "I'm offering the thing you most desire. A chance to start fresh. A clean slate."

"Why?" If there was one thing I'd learned, it was that nothing was simply *free*.

"Because the leader of the Vanir cannot be encumbered. The ruler of the realm must be unbound. Don't you know who I am now?"

I frowned. "No idea."

"Silly girl. You've been looking for me. And now that I'm finally here, you don't recognize me?"

I stared at the crone, completely confused.

She grinned, revealing a row of gray teeth. "Think hard, dearie. You're a clever girl."

Finally, it clicked in my mind. "Ah. You're a Norn? A weaver of Wyrd?"

The crone nodded. "You look chilled. I'll brew some tea that will warm your bones." She unslung the rucksack. Dropping the bag next to her, she slowly lowered herself to the gravel and pointed at the misty grass. "Sit just there. I'll pour."

I took my place opposite her, crossing my legs. With a

skeletal finger, she traced *kaun*. Instantly, flames sprang up from the stones by her side.

The Norn dug into her bag, retrieving a small, cast-iron teapot and a pair of old mugs. She placed the teapot on top of the fire, then with spider-like fingers scribed a rune I hadn't seen before. The pot hissed with steam as water filled it.

Then, she dug around in her rucksack until she found a leather pouch. From it, she dropped a handful of herbs into one of the mugs, then handed it to me.

Steam began to rise from the teapot, and she poured the boiling water into my cup. "I'm ready to sever the bond whenever you are. The link between your soul and Galin's."

I felt a strange twisting in my heart that I didn't really understand. But this was what I wanted. Wasn't it? "Really?"

She reached again into her rucksack. This time, she withdrew a ball of gray yarn the same color as her dress, as well as a silver pair of scissors.

I stared at the scissors. If the connection was severed, I could be master of my own destiny. I'd know if I actually loved him or if it was simply magic that drew me to him.

I'd be able to focus on freeing the Night Elves. And as Empress of the Vanir, I'd be able to protect them. They could come to Vanaheim. I'd seen the open plains, the vast forests—there was plenty of room. My brethren could soak in the warm sun, run their hands through the prairie grasses, breathe in the scent of the ancient trees. Under my protection, they would be free, safe, and happy.

I could truly be the North Star, for both the Vanir and the Night Elves.

But what was it that made me hesitate? Why hadn't I already told her to cut that thread? Was the Wyrd fighting back even now?

"Leading a people always requires great sacrifice," said the Norn quietly. "Your duty is bigger than you are. There are great snarls in the Wyrd for you to untangle; both your peoples need your full attention if they are to survive."

I looked at the ball of yarn in her hand and at the razor-sharp scissors in the other.

"Cut me free," I said.

The Norn smiled, and again, I saw gray teeth the color of death. Then, she raised the ball of yarn, drew out a single strand, and snipped it off.

I gasped as a great sense of hopelessness lanced through my heart, a shattering sense of loss. It was like nothing I'd ever experienced. Worse than my imprisonment in the Audr Mines, worse than being eaten by Nidhogg. It felt worse, even, than the deaths of my parents.

Had I just made a terrible mistake?

Never in my life had I felt so alone.

CHAPTER 44

ALI

The mist dissipated, and I found myself once again standing in the stone circle with the Regent, grief splintering my chest.

"Where did you go?" he asked, looking at me strangely.

"To see the Norn."

The Regent frowned, looking perplexed. "The fairies needed to meet you, but they have come and gone. They will return later to give you their blessing. They remember you fondly and are hoping you have new music for them. Apparently, they're getting tired of singing some song called 'Halo.'"

I smiled. "I have a new one they're going to love."

"They've disappeared for now. We must come back later."

He led me back through the forest, and as we walked, I asked him all about the realm. I learned that the Vanir weren't completely united. Though I was the Empress, thousands of years ago, they'd broken into four main clans. Various clans and factions complicated things further.

"Keeping them all in line," the Regent explained, "is going to be a full-time job."

"There must be a significant risk of assassination if it gets you the crown," I said. "How do I know that someone won't leap over the table, stab me in the heart, and declare himself new Emperor of the Vanir?"

"A Vanir can't rise against a crowned Empress or Emperor. That was why the coronation was important. You were able to kill the Emperor because you were not Vanir. You will be at risk around High Elves, or Night Elves. You will be at risk during the final battle of the Winnowing. You will fight the leader of the High Elves, and you must win at all costs. If you do not, Gorm could rule over us all."

And here was my chance to save the Night Elves. To become the North Star at last.

All I had to do was kill Gorm.

CHAPTER 45

GALIN

A sense of loss ripped through me. It wasn't just sadness; it was more like a deep foreboding. A painful drumming in my heart, like something terrible had happened but I hadn't yet found out what it was.

And then it struck me like an arrow to my heart. Ali had untethered our threads. Somehow, she must have found the Norn. Unless she'd died?

For minutes, I lay paralyzed. I felt as if my soul had been severed from my body once again, or at least part of it. Panic nearly drove me mad as I thought she could be dead, but Ganglati kept telling me she wasn't, that her soul was not with him.

It took me a few minutes to master control of myself once more, to think of Ali.

Even if she was no longer my mate, even if our threads had been ripped apart, I still had to save her. Fate or not, I loved her. And I had the wand. The power of the gods was finally in my grasp.

I held Levateinn, ready to scribe a portal spell.

As I did, though, I felt Ganglati's presence floating

through my mind, confusing me. Whispering in my thoughts. *You must finish what you started, Galin. You must complete the sacred task.*

"Not now, Ganglati. I need to see Ali."

And yet he was seizing control of me. Anger rippled through me. My wand hand continued to move, but it wasn't me tracing the runes. A portal expanded in front of me and Ganglati forced me into it. When I stepped out the other side, I found myself in Hela's throne room.

Fury simmered. Shades drifted around the dark stone, and votive candles flickered in ancient alcoves. Directly in front of me rested the remains of Hela herself. The body of the goddess reclined on a crumbling stone throne, a spindly crown on her head. Her dry, leathery skin was stretched tightly over her bones. One half of her face was faded blue, while the other gleamed like fresh bone. She seemed to grin at me, her lips peeled back over moldering teeth.

I gritted my teeth, wishing that I'd thought this promise through better. This was not the time to raise gods.

But I had seen my future—that I would be king. This was the path the Norns had woven for me. Perhaps this was a necessary step.

I lifted Levateinn, and the silver wand simmered with powerful magic—once wielded by Hela's father, Loki himself.

I shivered. Around me, the temperature dropped as shades swooped in to watch. I brought down the wand, then twisted my wrist to scribe *yr*—the rune for life.

A stream of silver magic unspooled from the end of Levateinn. It struck the dead goddess in the center of her chest, spreading over her like liquid metal. It didn't drip downwards as a normal fluid would. Instead, it flowed in all directions, along her arms, under her dress. It pooled at her feet even as it slid up her neck.

Around me, the shades whispered with growing excitement.

Liquid silver continued to flow from the end of Levateinn, washing over the goddess now, seeming to bathe her in metal. I stared, awestruck as the magic began to work. A strange elation filled my heart at the idea that a god would be alive again.

The movement began in her feet—the frozen muscles of the goddess's toes unclenching. Next were her fingers, trembling on the arms of the obsidian throne. Still, it came as a surprise when her entire body moved. A giant spasm that threw her head back against the throne.

"Yes!" screamed Ganglati, floating next to me. "My queen returns."

I clutched Levateinn with all my strength, staring at what was unfolding before me. The stream of silver had become a rush of power that filled the desiccated goddess with magic.

Hela's corpse spasmed again, and again, until she was literally thrashing on her throne. Around me, the shades were shouting, their wispy bodies twisting and churning in the air. They surrounded their queen until all I could see was the occasional shimmer of silver beneath their frantically hovering forms. Magic vibrated over the room.

Then, suddenly, the shades went still, hanging in the air. I heard a noise that iced my heart: a deep, rattling gasp that grew louder and louder. The first breath of a goddess who'd been dead a thousand years.

The gods are alive again.

And yet I couldn't linger here. I needed to get to Ali.

Hela sucked in a second breath, and with it, the shades spun in a terrible gyre, round and round like the whorl of a fearsome tornado.

Shivers ran up my spine at the wonder I was witnessing here, awe stilling my breath. I could see the goddess now.

Her skin softened as she inhaled the shades. Then, she opened her eyes and fixed me with her dazzling gaze.

She was beautiful in an eerie way—blue, swirling tattoos covering one half of her face, her skin pale as ice on the other side. She had delicate features, and her body glowed with a pearly light. Her dark hair fell over her robe, her body now gleaming with silvery light.

She stared at me, beautiful and terrifying at the same time, and I wanted to fall to my knees. When she held out her hand, my mind went blank.

"You, my king, have brought me back to life. Just as the Norns foretold. Rule with me here. Rule as king."

I went completely still, and I felt my heart stop for a moment. A horrible realization shattered my mind. I almost felt as though reality was crumbling around me. *This* was where I was supposed to rule as king? Not Midgard?

This was the fate the Norns had woven for me?

My fists tightened, and I shook my head. How could I defy a goddess? And yet I must.

Even as the darkness closed in around me, I knew I could not stay. Ali wasn't here. I had to make sure she was okay. I had to travel to Vanaheim and find her.

Before the goddess could stop me, I scribed the necessary runes, and a portal opened. I dove through it.

I fell hard onto the grasses of Vanaheim as the portal snapped shut behind me.

CHAPTER 46

ALI

One by one, my new Vanir warriors slipped through the portal. They were armed with sabers—a proper show of force for their new Empress.

The magic crackled as I stepped through, the last to arrive, and I found myself on the icy stone steps of the Citadel's amphitheater. Dark magic covered the Well of Wyrd, and the seating had been divided into two sections. One for the Vanir, one for the High Elves. The two tribes crowded onto the stone steps, waiting for the final battle.

The Night Elves were likely back in the caverns already, waiting for death. I wouldn't let it happen.

This *had* to work, or we'd be destroyed.

I surveyed the scene. Directly across from the Vanir section was the royal dais, perched just on the edge of the black lid of the well. In the center, Revna stood dressed in an emerald gown.

So, she'd survived. Disappointing.

And for some bizarre reason, she was wearing Gorm's crown.

I kept to the shadows, out of view, hiding behind the Vanir. I'd have the element of surprise on my side.

But what the fuck had happened to Gorm? I caught the Regent's attention, then nodded at Revna.

He nodded, understanding my meaning. "Where is King Gorm?" he shouted.

Revna adjusted her crown. "King Gorm has been murdered. As his only surviving child, I am now Queen of the High Elves. I shall defeat the Vanir. Once I do so, my first act as queen will be total extermination of the Night Elves."

Icy rage flickered through me. *I will rip your fucking head off.*

Where in Hel was Galin, though?

It was time to set my plan in motion. I nodded at the Regent, and he stepped forward. "We propose a battle of champions—a duel would be best. The winner becomes the leader of all the elves."

"Fine," Revna replied primly. "As is the ancient custom of the High Elves, I will be choosing a champion."

Disappointing. I'd hoped to kill her myself.

She smiled serenely, then held out her hand. The ground shook as a giant of an elf crossed onto the top of the stairs of the arena. He genuinely looked part giant—a wall of muscle, gripping a sword that was as large as I was. He had to be eight feet tall at least, his head disturbingly misshapen.

"You may choose your champion," she simpered.

"Oh, no," said the Regent. "Our Empress has said that she wishes to defend the realm herself."

I stepped out from behind my men, standing next to the Regent.

Revna sputtered. "*You?*"

"None other." I grinned. "Seems like we've both been promoted in the last twelve hours."

The crowd began murmuring, the High Elves clearly scandalized.

But where the fuck was Galin? If Gorm was dead, he should be king now, not his sister. Then this would all be over.

Gripping Skalei, I crossed out into the arena. The giant was huge, but all it would take was one well-aimed toss to his aorta. One throw, and my nightmare would finally be over.

Already, he was running for me, his sword carving through the air. He growled as I dodged him. Once. Twice. I'd stay out of his reach, dancing over the cold stone until the time was *just* right to throw Skalei.

I kept my eye trained on his neck, exactly where I needed to throw it, and let loose. The blade arced out of my hand, glinting in the light of the moon. But just at that moment, he swung for me, and the blade caught him in the collarbone, not where I needed it.

He screamed anyway, charging for me.

"Skalei."

With the blade in my hand again, I leapt into the air over his sword, driving Skalei at his chest. This was what I'd trained for all my life.

This time, Skalei met her mark perfectly, and the giant stopped, stunned. He staggered back, the ground shaking. Skalei protruded from his chest, and although he pulled her out, blood was now pouring from him. He stumbled, and I knew that the Night Elves would not die. I'd won.

With the High Elves vanquished, they would be under my control. I would lead them, the Vanir, and the Night Elves alike. All three tribes under my control. I'd create a glorious kingdom for us all.

Pure elation bubbled through me.

I just needed the *coup de grace*, and it would all be over.

"Skalei." With the hilt in my hand, I slammed her into his skull, and he dropped to the ground dead.

I felt myself beaming with victory. I'd done it. I'd fucking done it. With me as ruler, the Night Elves would be free. Elation pulsed through my body.

"No!" Revna screamed, ripping me out of my victory haze. "She cannot win. She's in league with Galin. She helped the king-slayer!"

I tore my eyes away from my opponent as he lay dying. Fury ignited in my body. Should I just kill her now?

Then, I felt the electrical rush of magic, and my gaze flicked to my right. A black portal was opening, not far from me.

Galin. His golden form was coming through. This felt like a miscalculation, somehow. He was in danger here, and I wanted to keep him safe.

"She killed the king!" Revna was ranting, completely out of her mind. "My spies told me!"

The crowd was roaring. And when I looked back at Revna, my heart skipped a beat. A fresh wave of dread crashed into me.

She held a crossbow aimed directly at me, ready to shoot.

"Skalei." I felt the blade in my hand again.

But the bolt was already on its way.

The world fell silent as Galin charged in front of me, taking the hit for me. The arrow slammed into his neck, tearing it open.

It was as if I was in a void, and everything was happening too fast for me to put my own thoughts into words. I knew I was screaming, but I couldn't hear a thing. Rage and pain ripped my mind apart, and I threw Skalei with all my strength.

The blade landed in Revna's forehead, and she slumped to the ground, blood pouring from her skull.

I looked down at Galin. Desperately I hoped he was only wounded, but his gaze was already lost in another realm. I fell to my knees. Blood gushed from the wound as I cradled him in my arms. Tears filled my eyes, the loss like shards of glass in my heart.

I was dimly aware of the Vanir rejoicing in our victory, not giving a shit about Galin. But my focus was on him. His golden eyes were unfocused now, his breath labored. He seemed like he was already far away, drifting into Valhalla, the glorious afterworld for those who died in battle.

The soul bond might be severed, but what I felt now was real. I had no question of that anymore. I pulled him up close, wishing desperately that I knew the magic he did. I'd be able to fix his ravaged throat. But all I knew was how to use a fucking knife.

The world dimmed around me, the roars of the crowd fading. His lifeblood was pumping out, his breath slowing. Panic screamed in my mind.

There was only him and me.

And ... Loki's wand on the stone by his side.

Loki's wand that could open worlds, raise the dead. Loki's wand, which I didn't know how to use—yet.

His eyes were going dim. A wand like that could bring someone alive again.

Before anyone could see what lay in front of me, I snatched up the wand and slid it up my sleeve. Then, I cradled Galin in my arms once more. I would find a way to bring him back.

But as I held him close, his body started to shimmer away, then simply disappeared into the shadows.

I stared at my empty arms, feeling like someone had torn my heart out.

I didn't know where he was, but I'd never seen a body disappear like that. Some strange magic was at work.

There it was again, that little spark of hope. That fleck of light in the darkness. Perhaps he'd managed to escape death again, like he always did.

And if so, Loki's wand would help me find him.

CHAPTER 47

GALIN

I'd always assumed that when my time came, I would accept it, allow fate to follow its course. But as I looked into Ali's eyes, I knew I had to fight it.

I was supposed to be King of the High Elves. I was supposed to be the one to usher in a new era, a golden age where the High Elves ruled with justice and morality.

Instead, I'd been shot in the neck by my own sister, and I found myself drifting in the astral plane. Death in battle meant Valhalla. I wondered what that might be like now, after Ragnarok.

But maybe it wasn't Valhalla I needed.

What if I could live? Hela had said I would rule as king.

I had one last deal to strike, and as I let myself drift through the astral plane, I summoned the shade.

Ganglati's voice rose in my mind. *Hela wants you by her side. She believes you will reign as king of Helheim.*

"Tell her I will accept her deal." For now. "But I stay alive. I keep my body, my beating heart. I keep my memories and my soul."

But Ali was my true fate. And even if I could feel that

she'd managed to sever our entwined threads—even if we were no longer mates—Ali was the beginning and the end for me. Soul bond or not, I loved her. Not Hela.

What was the price, I wondered, for betraying a goddess?

I snapped back into my body. Warm blood filled my mouth, and my thoughts drifted back to another time, when the gods had been alive and the verdant lands had spread out around us. I felt myself flickering between life and death.

For one moment, swords clashed around me, mountains rose into the mist, and thunder rolled over the horizon. The great mead hall of Valhalla rose above me, the place I'd always yearned to see, with a ceiling made of shields and the scent of roasted boar floating through the air. The final resting place of the Sword of the Gods; a realm that called to my soul. And I could stay there, forever, in the magnificent battle of the dead.

But that wasn't what I truly wanted. Not yet. I wanted Ali.

And that meant striking a deal. So, I was on my way to Helheim once more—the afterlife for those who died ingloriously. I would sit on an obsidian throne, with a black crown on my head, surrounded by gloom and shades. But I would keep my beating heart. And I would find my way to Ali again.

My soul drifted on psychic winds in a stygian darkness. It snapped back into my body, now fully healed. Frowning, I touched my throat where the arrow had ripped it open. Not even a scar to mar my skin.

A floor of gray stone spread out beneath me, and violet candlelight cast dancing shadows back and forth over the room.

My eyes flicked up, and there, I saw her reclining on her throne—Hela. Resplendent in all her glory, she shone with divine light. When she saw me, she tilted her head back and smiled. Her smile was stunning and terrifying at the same time, and I felt her dark power slide down to my very bones.

Her magic rumbled over the room like thunder, eyes gleaming black as onyx. My breath left my lungs.

A living goddess before me.

I fell to my knees. "I hail the goddess of the harrowing, Lady of Death, daughter of Loki. Wielder of famine and disease, mistress of death in beds of straw. Thank you for accepting me as a living liege in your court of death."

"Rise, Sword of the Gods." Her deep voice echoed off the walls. "You have brought me back to life. For this, you will rule with me as king."

I stood, momentarily awed by her as I looked into her impenetrably black eyes.

Already, though, I was thinking of how I could get back to Ali.

Perhaps this was what Wyrd had written for me, and this was the kingdom where I was meant to rule. But I would fight this fate with all my strength.

I was going to forge a new fate. And once that was done, I was going to do whatever it took to win back my mate.

CHAPTER 48

ALI

Barthol was silent as he walked beside me, running his fingers through the waist-high grass. "Is this really real, Ali?"

"Yes, it is."

Barthol shook his head in disbelief, and I understood the sentiment. A few hours ago, he'd been living underground—then he'd stepped through a portal into another world.

After serving him some venison stew, I'd led him along the river path, into the vast plains. Intermittently, a breeze would build into a little gust, and the grass would blow and sway like waves on a golden sea. As we walked, grasshoppers leapt for us, and pale-blue butterflies flitted in the air. Overhead, birds soared in a powder-blue sky. Beautiful, and perfect, and hard to enjoy at all without Galin here by my side.

Barthol stopped, turning to look at me. "I just can't quite believe you're actually an Empress."

My throat was tight. "Turns out I was always destined to become the North Star, just not in the way Mom expected."

"So, does this make me a lord?" He cracked a grin.

I think he'd expected me to say *No, of course not*, but I

CHAPTER 48

wasn't in the mood for moderation, so instead I said, "Sure. If you'd like, I can dub you Barthol, Lord of the Drunken Goats."

He laughed. "Would that come with a lifetime supply of mead?"

"Of course, dear brother. And all the goat milk you can drink, too."

Barthol shook his head. He'd started to turn back to the vista of grass when his eyes fell on Levateinn at my hip. "And that's *the* wand?"

"Yes."

He whistled low. "Can you make it do magic?"

I knew Galin could, and that he should be here. "Not yet. But I'm going to learn. I have a very important task. I have to find the prince."

"Let me have a go …" Barthol reached for the wand.

I slapped his hand away. "Too dangerous."

He narrowed his eyes. "You really don't trust me. Then you should try it."

I heaved a sigh. Carefully, I unclipped the wand from my belt. Based on its shimmering silver color, I'd expected it to be heavy and awkward, but it was surprisingly light and well balanced.

"Stand back," I said to Barthol.

Then, I waved the wand around in front of me with a few delicate strokes, as if I was conducting an orchestra.

Nothing happened. I shrugged. "I have no idea what I'm doing. I need Galin. Except, I can't get to him unless I learn how to use it."

Barthol gave me a pitying look, and I knew what he was thinking.

"He's still alive," I snapped.

He held up his hands. "I didn't say anything."

CHAPTER 48

"You were thinking it." I bit my lip. "Wait, I might have an idea."

I waved the wand again. I'd seen Galin inscribe the fire spell lots of times, and I was pretty sure I remembered how he'd done it. I said *kaun* under my breath as I traced the shape of the rune with the end of the wand.

For a moment, nothing happened, until I felt a sort of heaviness in the wand and a building of pressure along my arm. Then, for the briefest of seconds, a tiny flame appeared in the air, three feet in front of me. I grinned, hope stirring again.

"Amazing," said Barthol awstruck.

I stared at the wand. I had done magic. I *could* do magic.

And that mattered more than anything right now.

Because even if I'd severed our soul bond, I still felt like Galin was connected to me. And if he were dead, I'd simply know it. I'd feel it down to my bones, and blood, and every nerve in my body. But he was a part of me, and he was alive. Somewhere.

And I was going to do everything in my power to find him.

ALSO BY C.N. CRAWFORD

For a full list of our books, check out our website.
https://www.cncrawford.com/books/

And a possible reading order.
https://www.cncrawford.com/faq/

ACKNOWLEDGMENTS

Thanks especially to Christine all her edits and assistance. Bella and Jen both contributed to the extensive editing and polishing that got this book ready for publication. Carlos made us another beautiful cover. And last but not least, thanks so much to our advanced reader team for their help, and to C.N. Crawford's Coven on Facebook!

Printed in Great Britain
by Amazon